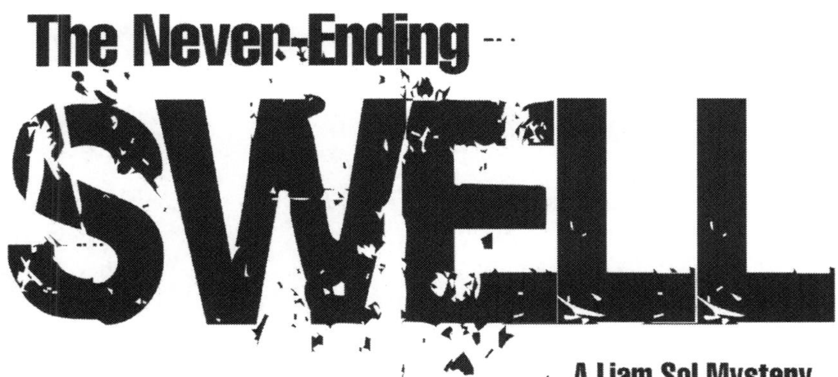

A Liam Sol Mystery

TIMOTHY BURGESS

THE NEVER-ENDING SWELL: A Liam Sol Mystery

Published by Station Square Media
16 West 23rd Street, 4th Floor
New York, NY 10010

This novel is a work of fiction. Any references to real people, events, establishments, organizations, or locales are intended only to give the fiction a sense of reality and authenticity, and are used fictitiously. All other names, characters, places, and incidents portrayed in this book are the product of the author's imagination.

Editorial: Write to Sell Your Book, LLC
Cover Design: Lisa Hainline
Interior Design: Steven Plummer
Production Management: Janet Spencer King

Printed in the United States of America for Worldwide Distribution.

ISBN: 978-0-9864206-3-4
Epub editions:
Mobi ISBN: 978-0-9864206-4-1
Epub ISBN: 978-0-9864206-5-8

First Edition
10 9 8 7 6 5 4 3 2 1

For Karen,

If not for you . . .

ACKNOWLEDGEMENTS

IT'S TRUE THAT writing—and staring at that damn blank screen—can be a lonely process. Fortunately for me, I was never really alone. So I want to give a big thank you to:

My wife, Karen; my brother, John Burgess; and my friends Jennifer Taw and Debra Ono for their excellent suggestions and numerous red flag alerts. They went way above the call of duty and their help was more than I could have hoped for.

The editorial team of Write to Sell Your Book: Brianna Flaherty, whose keen insights and suggestions made for a stronger story; and Diane O'Connell who calmly and expertly guided me through the entire publishing process of this book.

I never would have completed *The Never-Ending Swell* without the support and encouragement from the wonderful Ellen Snortland and her fantastic Writers' Workout Group.

Sadly, I am not a surfer, but Phil Bonney stepped up and kindly served as my surf consultant. He was very patient and supportive, even when I got things completely wrong. Any mistakes and errors in this book are all mine.

I was also lucky enough to have had a host of allies who kept me motivated throughout the writing of this book: Jennifer Zeller, Misti Barnes, Joan Aaresstad, JaBari Brown, Stella Lopez, Guy Margedant, Tony Perez, Charles Garcia, Dave Collins, Lisa Gaeta, James Vasquez, Paul Kikuchi, and my father-in-law Thomas Tombrello.

My daughters, Hayley and Kinsey, have always been supportive of their dad. Girls, you have no idea how much strength you have given me! This is for you!

Special shout-outs to my mother, Anne Burgess; my father, John Burgess Sr., whose stories kept me awake at night (I miss you, Dad!); and to my sister, Barbara Shaw.

LA BOLSA, SOUTHERN CALIFORNIA, 1967

CHAPTER ONE

THE WINDS AND storms are far away. You never see them. They push the water over the Pacific and across the markers of time. They get help from the eternal rhythmic pull of the moon, and the ocean floor, and the gods. They keep pushing, collecting power until the waves they've begotten are lined up for the final sprint before it all ends on a sandy beach. You're sitting on your board facing the ocean, waiting, knowing they're coming. Even though you've done this countless times, your heart still races as you see the wave begin to take shape. You turn and start paddling, feeling the power and the speed of the water trying to overtake you. Looking over your shoulder, you position yourself in the wave. Timing and direction are everything. In one swift motion you push yourself up on your feet, and you're on top of the wave. You race down its face, the velocity increasing, your blood pumping hard like jet fuel surging through your veins. You're on the edge now, close to losing control, but you're focused, completely in tune with whatever may come. As you reach the bottom you turn back into the wave. You put your back foot at the end of your board and place your hand into the wall of water, stalling to let the curl catch up to you. You're the bullet in the barrel now, the eye of the storm. You're flying through a kaleidoscope of countless forms of greens, blues, and whites swirling all around you until you shoot out of the tunnel and into the morning sun. The world is laid out before you, fresh and alive. You're stoked. No matter how many times you've done this, you smile: there's no better way to start the day.

I was surfing the south side of the wooden pier at La Bolsa Beach, but got out of the water just as the daily rush of tourists arrived. Like clockwork, they settled in at eleven in the morning, each summer day, as reliable as the swallows returning to San Juan Capistrano. Most of the surfers moved to the north side of the pier—it didn't have snack stands, restrooms, or lifeguards, but the break and the beach were ours. The north beach was hidden from Pacific Coast Highway by steep cliffs. The day-trippers couldn't spot the beach from the road; either they didn't think one existed there, or it took too much climbing to make an afternoon at the beach worthwhile. I'd usually head north of the pier to continue surfing, but I had to have lunch with my father. I'd rather have kept surfing, but long ago I'd learned never to say no to him.

I hauled my surfboard up the beach, dodging past a couple of kids skimboarding along the shore, and wove my way through the crowd of beachgoers. The scent of Coppertone hung in the air like cigarette smoke. Transistor radios were tuned to Boss Radio or similar sounding stations, all blasting out the latest hits with disc jockeys talking so fast you got out of breath just listening to them. Families were laying out their beach towels and taking sandwiches and cans of Coke from Styrofoam ice chests. Little kids were running down to the water with tiny buckets and toy shovels, eager to make sandcastles. I got a few smiles and looks from some of the girls on the beach. I didn't know them, but it didn't matter—they smiled at any surfer who walked by. The girls thought of us as some exotic species and they couldn't wait to tell their girlfriends back in the valleys about their encounters with us.

I smiled at a pretty blonde who looked like a teenaged version of Brigitte Bardot. She returned the smile, but her father gave me the look, so I kept on walking. Living here, you get used to the look. Stay away. I found it funny that families would drive miles to La Bolsa, my home, and then look at me as if I was the one who didn't belong.

As I lifted my board into the bed of my Chevy Fleetwood, the blonde from the beach walked up to me. She had the fresh face of a girl who didn't live at the beach, the kind of girl who didn't yet know what she wasn't supposed to know. Her skin was tan and dotted with just a few freckles, and her lips were touched with a trace of salt from the ocean. I imagined they'd be very nice to kiss. I glanced behind her, expecting to see her father running at me with a sawed off shotgun, but if he was around, I couldn't see him.

She smiled. "Don't worry. He thinks I'm getting a Coke at the snack stand."

"I wasn't worried."

She tilted her head a bit and sized me up with her eyes.

"You weren't?"

I let out a short laugh. "I'm pretty fast. I think I can outrun him."

"But can you outrun a bullet?"

I paused. I wasn't sure if she said it as a joke or not. I'd had a few run-ins with fathers before, and they never ended well.

"He can get a little protective of me when it comes to boys." She gave me a look and smiled. "I mean men."

"I'm not that much older than you. I'm only 24."

"That kind of makes you a man, doesn't it?"

"I guess." I scanned the beach behind her. "Just how protective does your dad get?"

"Don't worry. He's all bark and no bite."

"I guess I'm going to have to take your word on that."

She laughed. It wasn't a giggle, but a strong laugh that came from her gut. I liked that.

"Liam Sol. Nice to meet you."

I extended my hand. She took it. She had a firm grip for a girl, and her hand was soft. I liked the combination.

"Cindy Shaw. Nice to meet you as well." She blushed and I liked that, too.

Cindy told me that she lived in Bakersfield and was spending Labor Day weekend in La Bolsa with her parents. She'd be starting college in Santa Barbara in just a few weeks. She said she couldn't wait to leave home so she could get on with her life.

"I was watching you out there. You're pretty good." The blush hadn't yet faded from her skin.

I smiled. I liked my chances. Any worries about her father faded away as she was too pretty to pass up. We chatted a bit longer and arranged to meet later that night at the corner of Main and Pacific Coast Highway. A great wave and a beautiful girl—maybe there were better ways to live, but I doubted it.

CHAPTER TWO

I MET MY FATHER for lunch at the La Bolsa Beach Club. Mexicans weren't allowed to be members of the club, but since my dad owned the land on which it stood, they kindly made an exception for him.

My father was seated by a window that overlooked the ocean. He was going through some papers, probably something to do with the man-made marina he wanted to build, a place where the rich could park their fancy yachts. He'd been battling the city for years over the planned marina, and it looked like it was finally going to be approved. Many of my fellow surfers didn't want the marina built as they were concerned about the effect it might have on the beach and our city. I honestly hadn't given it much thought.

My father was, as usual, wearing a perfectly tailored dark suit. He believed that people did, in fact, judge a book by its cover, so he made a point to always be the best dressed person in the room. I didn't get it. Heck, I didn't even own a suit. I was wearing Levi's, and a white oxford shirt with the sleeves rolled up, and Keds tennis shoes.

My father put the papers in his briefcase, stood up, and smiled, extending his hand. He had a strong, muscular grip, and he expected you to respond likewise. Long ago he had taught me the importance of a good handshake and what it could tell you about the other person. I got the firm handshake part down, but reading anything into one was still lost on me. The things he understood. I hoped that one day I'd know what he knew and what it all meant. Over lunch we engaged in some father-son small talk: football, LBJ, and Vietnam. He told me the marina had a few more hurdles to clear before final approval, but he was optimistic. My father always spoke in a formal manner, almost forced and self-conscious, as though if his true voice ever came out, people might think less of him.

I noticed him sneak a smile at the pretty hostess who strolled by our table, her face turning a soft shade of pink. Women, it didn't matter what age, found my father attractive. With his muscular build from working out with weights every morning, his perfectly cut hair, and his neatly trimmed mustache, he could have given Hugh Hefner a run for his money. After the hostess passed us, my father's expression shifted to a sort of grimace, as if he didn't like what he was thinking.

"So, Liam, are you currently seeing anyone?"

Here we go again, I thought.

"No one serious," I said.

"Have you heard from Dawn lately?"

I tensed up. "You know I don't like talking about her."

"You never should have let her go."

"I didn't let her go; she left me." Dawn had been my girlfriend from junior high school through college. My sister Isabelle told me that Dawn had kept me from being like everyone else, that she brought out the things that made me special. Isabelle said things like that, but I never believed her.

"We all liked her," my father said. "We want you to—"

When he saw my expression, he put his hands up in front of his chest.

"To what?" I asked.

He was about to respond when the waiter gave me a temporary reprieve.

"Will there be anything else?" The waiter asked.

My father looked at me, and I shook my head. I wanted to get out as fast as possible.

"Just the check, please," he said.

I regretted leaving an afternoon of great waves for this lunch, and I could tell that my father wasn't done with me. There was more he wanted to say, and I hoped to God he would leave well enough alone. The two of us had always gotten along. He'd taught me how to fish, swim, build a campfire—all the things that boys should know. Once I hit high school, he loosened the reins; but he would let me know if I had gone too far, and he straightened me out when needed. He served as a good guide in life for me. I wanted him to be proud of me. And whenever I stared into his eyes, I searched for that certain sparkle that told me that he thought I was on the right track. This time, though, it felt different. His eyes examined me as if he were searching for some part of me that I tried to conceal from him—and even more unsettling, something that I might be hiding from myself.

"Liam, your mother and I are worried about you."

"No need to be. I'm doing great. Life is good."

"Perhaps it is my fault. I let you play for so long, hoping you'd finally get serious about life. Liam, all you do is surf and chase these young girls. You have your college degree. Don't you want to accomplish more than that?"

My parents had been more than patient. They had paid for my education, let me stay for free in a house they owned, and generally let me do as I wanted.

"I've got a job."

"You write for that little surf magazine. Is that a career? How much do they pay you?"

I shrugged. I didn't tell him that I was only a freelancer and the pay wasn't close enough to live on. Nor would competing in surf contests help, as there just wasn't much money to be made. There were cool sponsorship opportunities to be had, but I never pursued any of them. Mostly, I hated the idea of surfing as a competitive sport. Contests took away all that was pure and natural about surfing. It was no longer about the spirit that lived within the waves, but about performing for those to whom you willingly granted the power to judge you. These contests were a virus that infected the surf scene. And if you weren't careful, you'd find yourself worshipping at the feet of faceless salesmen, who offered you trinkets in exchange for your soul.

I couldn't hide from one truth, though. I damn well knew that without my father helping me out financially, I'd have to go out and find a real job, one where surfing would come a distant second in my life. I had no idea what I wanted to do when I grew up. It wasn't something that I liked to dwell on.

"Liam, you're 24 years old. You need to start thinking about becoming a man and start taking on some responsibilities."

I felt a jab in my gut. I didn't like where this conversation was going.

"I want you to come work for me. I can't run the company forever, and I'd love to train you and hopefully, someday, turn it over to you. You are a smart man, Liam. I want you to take over after, well, you know." He laughed. "When I'm ready to retire."

I couldn't imagine my dad ever retiring, and I couldn't imagine ever working for him. "What about Marie?"

"Your sister is smart—and tough—but she's a woman. This business is no place for her. Once she finds the right man, she'll want to be a mother, and then who will run the business?"

"I don't see Marie marrying anytime soon." Marie had little patience when it came to most men. She'd had only one boyfriend that I knew of, and after about a year of serious dating, she had crushed his heart. I almost think she enjoyed it.

"Yes, well, Marie and I have different ideas about which direction my company should go. I hope we can work it out."

I didn't want to tell him that all I wanted to do was surf. I couldn't imagine doing anything else.

"I know what you're thinking, but everything will be much easier for you. I have a lot of influence, and well, since your mother passed down her Irish genes to you, people have a hard time seeing that you're part Mexican. You won't have the same problems I faced—and still face."

I met his eyes. "I don't mind being part Mexican; it's being part Irish that's killing me."

My father let out a short laugh before turning serious again. "Liam, I want you to come work for me. I want to pass the company down to you like my father passed it down to me. It would mean a lot. And it's time."

It's time. The words stung.

I wanted nothing more than to please him. He was the finest man I knew, and it hurt to think that I had disappointed him. "I'll consider it," I told him, though I didn't mean a word of it.

"This is not something to think over. Your mother and I have discussed this. You will work for me. You can't live like this forever. Liam, you wouldn't have to give up surfing entirely, but you are too old to chase young girls around and live off of my good graces."

Where was this coming from? I wanted him to shut up. I didn't want his life. I wanted to live my life.

"You need to start paying your own way. It's what men do."

"Okay, I got it," I yelled.

"Liam!"

"I don't want to do what you do. Don't you understand that? I don't want to..."

"What?"

"Be you, okay? I don't want to be you!"

The dining room fell silent. My father's face turned red from what I was sure was a mixture of embarrassment and anger. He smiled and shrugged as if to indicate to the other diners that our argument was no big deal. I put my head down. I had never yelled at my father like that and never in public.

The waiter returned and placed the check softly on the table, trying hard not to be noticed. My father grabbed the check and read it over.

"I'm sorry," I said. And I was sorry, but I didn't like what he was saying—whether true or not, I wasn't ready to deal with it.

"I know you regret your outburst, but do not ever do that again." He observed me for a few seconds. "Don't think I don't believe in you, because I do. You'll do the right thing."

At this point, I didn't know if I would do the right thing or even if I would know what the right thing was.

After he paid the bill, we walked out to his car. He placed his hand on my shoulder and said something that made me pause. "You need to quit running away from life."

There are times when some truth is revealed to you and though you may deny it, it sticks in your brain and leaves you feeling a bit unsettled until the day comes when you can no longer avoid it. I couldn't face my father's gaze, so instead I put my head down and pretended to stare at my shoes.

"Get him out of here," my father yelled.

Startled, I raised my head and saw my father pointing his finger at Eddie Capuano. Eddie had his hand out, asking some of the club members for spare change. He was a bum, a harmless one, but he knew where the big money hung out. I doubted that this group would be very giving. He'd have better luck going back to the beach.

"Just get him off the lot."

Two security guys, big enough to play for the Los Angeles Rams, sprinted past us, grabbed hold of Eddie, and quickly escorted him down the long driveway.

"Let go of me," Eddie screamed. "I'm not hurting anyone."

My father shook his head and shouted after them, "Be gentle with him." And then he looked me dead in the eyes. "I want your answer soon." He gave me a couple of hard pats on the back and climbed into his waiting Cadillac.

As I watched his car disappear down the coast, I wondered how long I could put him off. Even though it was after one o'clock, the waves were holding up just fine as the usual onshore winds failed to show. I still had plenty of time to go home and grab my board. As I walked to my truck, I was surprised to find that I felt more than a little ashamed of myself.

CHAPTER THREE

MY LITTLE HOUSE sat back from the cliffs, across the road from the ocean, on the corner of Golden Sun Pass and Pacific Coast Highway. My home was nestled next to a couple of oil wells, large metal prehistoric birds endlessly bobbing for black gold, squeaking without end, night and day. Beyond the sounds of the oil wells, across the highway, I could hear waves crashing on the beach. The sounds coming from both the ocean and the machines were never in sync—each were led by a different conductor. And tonight, as I lay in bed, their symphonies sounded like a funeral procession leading a flotilla of lost surfers off the edge of the world.

I could still smell Cindy's perfume on the pillow. I'd driven her back to her hotel just after midnight, and she had fought back her tears the entire way. I put my arm around her and asked if she was okay. Cindy turned away from me and gazed out the side window of my truck. She no longer resembled a younger version of Brigitte Bardot. She was just a girl. I could tell she regretted everything. She realized that I was nothing but a big mistake, one she hoped to rid from her memory forever. She lied to her parents, cheated on her boyfriend, and, I think, lost her virginity to me. I told her everything she wanted to hear, so I could get what I wanted. And now I felt like shit. Maybe my dad was right. Maybe I was too old for this.

Remorse had given way to exhaustion when the phone rang. I let it ring a few times before I muttered a wary hello.

"Liam Sol?"

Whoever the caller was, he sounded upset. I hoped it wasn't Cindy's father calling to let me know that he was on his way over to put a bullet between my eyes.

"Liam, it's Dane Lohan."

Dane Lohan, the worst guard on our old high school basketball team, was now a detective with the La Bolsa Police Department. I hoped he never had to use his gun, because if he did, the only person who would be safe would be the guy he was trying to shoot. Dane and I weren't that close, and though we saw each other from time to time around town, we rarely said more than hello.

He told me to meet him down at the beach. I asked why, and when he told me, I sat up on the bed, unable to move until I heard Dane ask, "Liam, are you still there?" I hung up and held the pillow close to my chest. The scent of Cindy's perfume still lingered in my room, and I realized there were so many things I wanted to take back.

I threw on some clothes and left the house. There was no need to rush, and maybe if I took my time, somehow, magically, everything would turn out to be all right. I walked along PCH toward downtown La Bolsa. My stomach churned. I didn't want to see what they wanted me to see. I didn't think I could face it.

Lifeguard Station 3 stood just south of the pier, near Main Street. The night felt cool, almost chilly, and the fog had settled in. I buttoned up my Pendleton shirt and surveyed the ocean. The giant oil platforms were all lit up. They looked like battleships ready to storm the coastline. I saw the occasional dying bonfire on the beach. Curfews kept the kids at home, and the only folks out now were the police, bums, and maybe a couple of guys fishing from the shore. I saw the lights from police cars in the distance. I slowed my pace, suddenly scared of what waited for me on the beach. I passed Lovely Rita's Bikini Shop. Rita was allergic to the sun, but she couldn't imagine living anywhere but the beach. I saw a light on above her shop, and I imagined her in her apartment drinking mint tea, lost in an obscure novel from somewhere like India. The scent of cinnamon-tinged incense drifted down from her open window.

I glanced into Gary's Surf Shop to see if I could spot the board he was shaping for me. All I saw were new boards from bigger manufacturers squeezing out his originals. Gary, blind in one eye, still shaped his boards by hand. He could size you up in a second and know exactly how to shape the very board you needed. He never got it wrong.

I walked past Lou's Liquor to the Gold Coast, where I had seen Dick Dale wail on his guitar, whipping the crowd into a frenzy. Sadly, Dick's music seemed to have fallen out of favor lately. I crossed Main Street and saw the Crest Theater where crowds of locals came to watch surf movies every Tuesday night. A few doors down from that was The Belly of the Whale bar, where in the late afternoon we'd share pitchers of beer and look out the big open-air windows and watch the girls stroll by in their bikinis.

La Bolsa seemed to be an underachieving city, never daring to compete with the fancier towns like Newport and Laguna. The city was content to be a town of surfers, fishermen, small businesses, and a handful of farms. It didn't want to be anything more than a sleepy seaside town, but I'd heard my dad talk of wanting to modernize La Bolsa, to turn it into something to be proud of, whatever that meant. I crossed PCH, under a flickering streetlight, and then hesitated just before reaching the parking lot. I didn't want to take another step forward. I wanted to go back and crawl under my sheets. Then I'd wake up and all would be well.

There were about a dozen cops, their flashlights beaming down on the body. I swallowed hard and started running toward the lifeguard stand.

The sand felt as if it were trying to grab my feet, to keep me from reaching the body. When I got to the scene, Dane stopped me. He was a big guy—at six-foot-three, he stood a couple inches taller than me. He had the perpetual sunburn of someone who the sun didn't like very much.

"Liam, I'm sorry."

I pushed my way past him and stared down at the body. The cops stepped back, allowing me to get a good look.

"He washed up on shore around two a.m. A couple of fishermen found him," Dane said.

My father didn't look real to me. It was as if someone from the Movieland Museum had carved him from wax. His mouth was agape, as if frozen in a scream. His eyes were open, staring at nothing. My father looked weak and soft. Nothing like the man I knew. Nothing like the man I had just had lunch with. I felt ashamed. I wanted to cover him up so no one else could see him like this. I bent down, my head spinning, my mouth dry. I reached out and touched my father's face. It felt cold and swollen.

"Liam, don't touch him, please."

"What happened?"

Dane turned him over just a bit, revealing a knife stuck deep inside my father's back.

"We were hoping you could tell us."

It was as if every wave I ever surfed had crashed down on me at one time. I didn't know what was up or down. I stared at the ocean that had swallowed my father, and I felt as if I were seeing it for the very first time.

I was drowning. The water cradled me and kept me warm. Though I couldn't breathe, I was no longer scared. A fish swam by, beckoning me to follow, but my arms were dead tired from fighting the riptide. One moment I had been swimming and the next I had been dragged out to sea. I tried to make my way back, but the harder I tried, the farther out I found myself. I could barely make out the lifeguard tower; the shore was so far away, I knew no one could see me. I tried to yell out, but I just ended up swallowing the sea. I was alone and panic hit me. I tried to raise my arms and wave for help, but they were too heavy to lift. I fought to keep my head above water until I felt myself let go, and then I sank under the water. I didn't fight it; I welcomed it now. This was a calm I'd never experienced before. A soft light enveloped me, and I felt at home. I closed my eyes and started to slip into a soothing slumber, and then a warm hand grabbed me and took me away.

The sun blinded me, and I found myself lying on the sand, coughing up water. The hand still held me. Faces I had never seen loomed above, surrounding me. And then I saw him. My father. He looked down at me, smiling and concerned. The sun directly behind him, forming a halo around his head.

"You're okay, Liam. You're safe now."

He picked me up and carried me through the crowd of onlookers. I heard one of them say, "Did you see how fast he swam? He beat the lifeguards out there."

"I'm sorry," my father said to me. "I'm so sorry."

He wrapped me tighter in his arms and kissed my cheek. He swore nothing bad would ever happen to me again. And I knew nothing would. He was my father, and he would always be there to protect me. I was eight years old, and I knew he was telling the truth. My father would always be there for me.

Someone spoke to me, but they sounded far away. I opened my eyes and saw Dane standing next to me, but I couldn't make out a word he was saying. It sounded as if a hand had covered his mouth.

"What?"

"Your mother is okay," he said, his voice louder. "She's at the house, and Marie is with her. She said your dad left home around eleven and never came back."

I stared at my father. Water dripped from his clothes. While I knew he was dead, I couldn't help but inspect him for a sign of life, a breath, a movement, anything—but nothing came. There I was fooling around with a teenage girl while someone ran a knife into my father's back. I wondered if he could have seen my house from the water. What was he thinking as the last few drops of blood left his body? I knew no warm hand had been there to rescue him. One of the last things I had said to my father was that I didn't want to be anything like him. And while he took his last breath of life, I was talking a young girl out of her clothes.

"Did you hear me? Your mother is fine."

"I know, I know."

Dane looked at me as if I lived on a completely different planet from him. I didn't know why, but it never even occurred to me that she might be in danger.

"Marie said Isabelle was safe and sound as well and that she'd be at the house tomorrow. So, at least the rest of your family is okay."

I gave Dane a pat on the arm. "Thanks for checking on them."

Dane had always liked my oldest sister, Marie. He never mentioned it to me when we were in high school, but I knew. People talk. Still, I appreciated that he never tried to use me to get to her. Dane was okay, but he was someone who always chased things he'd never catch. And Marie would always be well beyond his reach.

"Do you have any idea who could have done this?" Dane asked.

"No. No one would want to kill him. No one."

"Well, somebody wanted to, and did."

He kept talking, but I wasn't listening. I read the current, trying to track how my father had made it to this part of the beach. "The pier," I told Dane. "He was killed on the pier."

"Huh? Oh, yeah, we're going to check that out. Liam, why don't you go be with your family now? They'll need you there, and we can talk more about this tomorrow." But I didn't want to go to the house. I didn't know what to do. I didn't know how to act. I didn't know what my mother and sisters expected of me.

"No. I can stay."

Dane put his hand on my shoulder. It felt cold, as if he'd just come out of a meat locker. "We're going to have to move the body and uh... it's police work. I don't think you want to be around for this. It can be pretty upsetting for the victim's family."

Victim. That's what my dad was now. He was no longer Felix Sol. He was a victim. And I was the victim's family. I walked back up toward the parking lot and heard one of the policemen asking, "How well did he know his father?" He said it like I didn't know a damn thing about him, like I didn't know what the hell I was talking about. A seagull flew over me, rushing away from the sea, its wings flapping furiously. I wondered if something were chasing it. I glanced behind me, but all I saw was a group of men leaning over my father's body. They looked like muggers dividing up the loot.

I didn't go home. I didn't go see my mother, even though I knew I should be at her side. Instead I walked south down PCH, all the way to La Bolsa Canyon, and then a few miles inland on one of the tiny canyon roads. I went to the home of the one person who had always been there for me. The one person I could talk to. The one person who truly knew me.

I sat on the curb, across the street from her small cottage. I didn't see her yellow VW Bug parked in the driveway. Dawn had been dating a new guy. She was probably with him now, in his arms, her head resting on his chest. She was there for him now, not for me. I'd let her go. I'd let her drift away. Dawn had once reached out to me at her most vulnerable moment, but I had been too frightened, too scared. I thought of one of the last things my father said to me: *You need to start thinking about becoming a man.*

I swallowed hard and felt the tears silently rush down my face. And I sat and waited for Dawn, yet hoping she wouldn't come home.

CHAPTER FOUR

MY FRIEND HIKE once said that he never trusted beautiful days. "When everything seems so perfect," he said, "that's when all hell is about to break loose, but because it's so damn pretty, no one ever notices until it's too late."

I thought about those words while hitchhiking up La Bolsa Canyon Road to my parents' house. I don't think I had ever seen a bluer sky or more beautiful waves. It was a day to be optimistic, a day to dream, a day, under normal circumstances, that you hoped would never end. Even the scent of the eucalyptus trees floating through the canyon seemed hopeful. Maybe last night had just been a bad dream. My father would be up at the hacienda right now, walking under the olive trees that he loved so much. As hard as I tried though, I couldn't fool myself. The image of my father's bloated body on the beach had seared itself into my soul. I wanted this day to end. I wanted to get to the part where it would all get better and where things would get back to normal. But maybe this was how life really was. Maybe I would no longer be able to hide from it.

Dawn never came home. I didn't know why I went to her house last night, or why I thought she could provide answers when I knew there were none, or why I felt so weak seeking the comfort I thought only she could administer. My dad always liked her. "She's good for you," he'd say.

After high school, before she left for college, we agreed that we should test our relationship and try seeing other people. It didn't work for either of us. Every holiday weekend and every summer, we'd end up in each other's arms, drawn together by something I couldn't understand.

During summer breaks we would park at the beach, sit in the back of my truck, and drink the Mexican beer that I could only find in the *mercados* of Santa Ana. As it grew dark, we'd make up our own constellations and talk about the novels we were required to read. She was one of the smartest people I knew. There were moments when I couldn't help but ask her if we were talking about the same books. While I loved the stories, I never could get the subtext. She'd laugh and tell me that I never tried to read between the lines, and she'd explain the symbolism to me better than any of my professors. Or maybe it was because when Dawn spoke, I listened.

My thumb hadn't been out that long when a dented, red, '64 Corvair Monza pulled up on the side of the road, kicking the dust up around me, making it hard to see. When the air cleared I saw a young Marine behind the wheel, smiling. As a surfer I'd experienced a few run-ins with Marines, usually at Trestles, but this guy was so fresh-faced and eager, it made the ride hard to turn down. That, and I was tired of walking.

"Where are you going?"

"Just a few miles up the road," I told him.

He reached over and opened the door for me. I don't know whether it came from his aftershave or something in the air, but as I entered the car, I caught the faint odor of rotten apples. I glanced at the interior, but it was empty—not a map, a scrap of paper, nothing. I was in no mood for a chat as I had been trying to brace myself for the visit home, but Private Adam Ricks liked to talk.

"You're a surfer?"

I nodded. Talking to a jarhead was the last thing I wanted to do.

"Must be nice. Must be nice."

I nodded again, and he went on to tell me he was from Idaho and had never seen the ocean until arriving for boot camp in San Diego. He wanted to know what it was like to ride the waves, and how cool it must be to live on the beach.

"There's nothing better in the world," I said.

"Must be nice," he said again with a smile on his face.

That's when he told me he was shipping out to Vietnam the next week. I recalled getting my notice a few months back. I'd showed it to my dad. He grabbed the letter from my hands and told me he'd look into it. There was a doctor he knew who might be able to help. I hadn't heard from the Selective Service since, and hopefully that'd be the end of it.

We were silent for a while, but I felt as if I should respond.

"You scared?" I asked.

"Nah. Heck, I enlisted."

"Why?" I couldn't even conceive of wanting to go to war, putting your life on the line for rice farmers, wanting to fight and kill people who did nothing to you—and that haircut, forget about that.

He gave me a strange look. "To answer the call of duty and fight for my country. To make the world safe for others. To stop the Commies from taking over the world. Why aren't you going?"

I felt the tension rise. There were a million ways I could have responded to him, but I came out with the first thing that crossed my mind.

"Because I don't have to."

His eyes held me for a second, sizing me up. He shook his head and didn't say another word to me until he dropped me off at the road that led up to my parents' home.

As I got out of the car, I saw Ricks staring up the road that led up to my house. He saw the orange groves, the rows of olive trees in the distance, and the size of the estate.

"Yep," he said, but his tone had changed. "Must be nice."

Private Adam Ricks looked as if the world suddenly made sense to him, and he didn't like what he saw. Life was indeed not fair. The same rules didn't apply to everyone. I came from a wealthy family, and he didn't. He was going to war, and I wasn't. I could see it in his eyes. He felt that people like him had been toiling in the dirt for people like me for years, making the world a better place for us, without even a word of thanks. That's the way it had always been, and that's the way it would always be.

I thanked him and watched him as he drove off, knowing he'd soon be in a war zone. I had no idea what drove people like Adam Ricks. He didn't wait for the draft board to call him. He signed up for the war all by himself. I couldn't imagine signing up for anything like that, nor could I understand why he believed he had the obligation to make the world safe for others. It made no sense. Just let me live my life, and you live yours—that is all I wanted. That's all I could ask for.

CHAPTER FIVE

I WALKED UP THE road to the house as I'd done a million times before, but now, somehow, I felt out of place. Something about the Marine had gotten to me, like a bad dream you can't shake. As I approached the house, every step I took felt shaky and unstable, as if the very soil in which I grew up was about to give way at any second.

The original part of the rancho had been built of adobe in the early 1800s. King Carlos III of Spain issued the land to Miguel Aldrete, an officer in the Spanish army. My grandfather, upon seeing the house and the land, had determined that this was what the American dream was all about. The owner didn't want to sell to a Mexican, but my grandfather told him that he would pay the full asking price, in cash. The man happily agreed to his terms. Money, my grandfather realized, was what made men convince themselves that they were doing the right thing.

I wanted to leave as soon as I walked into the house. There were at least two dozen people milling around, drinks in their hands, engaging in polite talk. No one noticed me, so I tried to slip away and find my mom. But my sister, Marie, intercepted me.

"Well, you finally showed up."

She gave me the once-over with her usual look of disdain.

"I see you've dressed for the occasion," she said.

I'd forgotten that I was wearing the same clothes from last night. I rubbed my chin and realized I needed a shave and a shower.

"It's good to see that Felix's death hasn't interfered with your surfing," she said.

It bothered me that she called Mom and Dad by their first names. I guessed that came as the result of Marie skipping childhood. Whether it was by design or because she found youth too trivial for her, I didn't know. As long as I could remember, she seemed to resent me. Perhaps because I was the youngest, maybe because I was the only son, maybe because she thought our parents let me get away with too much. Whatever the truth, I didn't care. I never understood why life had to be such a chore to Marie. It shouldn't have been. Marie was strikingly beautiful, with long black hair and green eyes in which most men would willingly let themselves drown. She could have had most anything in life, yet she'd chosen very little and was angry with the results.

"It's nice to see you, too, Marie. Where's Mom?"

"I don't know, but be careful with her," she warned. "Brona's being strong, but that's not going to last."

"Is Isabelle here yet?" Isabelle was the middle child. She lived with her husband, Glenn, in Beverly Hills.

"I don't know," Marie snapped. "But I have everything under control."

"I wasn't…" There was nothing to say. I nodded my head and gave her a peck on the cheek. Even then she tried to pull back.

"I'm going up to have a quick shower," I said.

She didn't move when I walked past her. As I climbed the stairs I tried to spot my mother, but I couldn't find her among the crowd.

They still kept my bedroom for me, though it was sparsely furnished—just a bed and a drawer filled with a few of my old clothes. Thankfully, I found some nice slacks and a decent shirt I could change into. After I showered and changed, I headed down the hall to the stairs, but stopped when I heard my mother's voice. She was arguing with someone. I walked to her room and stood outside the door, which was open just a crack, and tried to hear who she was with. It turned silent for a moment, so I slowly pushed the door all the way open. I saw my cousin, Carlos, the head field hand, seated in a chair, his head buried in his hands, my mother standing over him like a teacher scolding a troubled student.

"I don't think we have any more to say to each other." Her Irish brogue peaked when she got upset, and it was as thick now as I'd ever heard it. She'd lived most of her life in the U.S., but the accent could still get strong. "You can leave now."

Carlos rose from his chair but froze when he saw me. My mother turned and gave me a warm smile, as if she'd known I had been there all along. Carlos nodded his head, his eyes red and unfocused. He lowered his face and walked quickly out of the room. My mother gave me a warm hug. I smelled a mix of alcohol and Dentyne on her breath. She wasn't a drinker, but given what had happened to my father, I guessed it made sense.

"He wanted to talk about taking over for your father. Can you believe it?" She gave me another hug. "How are you, Liam? Are you okay?"

I told her I was fine and asked how she was doing.

"I couldn't tell ya," she said, shaking her head. "I can't believe it. I don't want to believe it."

My mother was a tall woman who liked using her height to her advantage. That, along with her penetrating blue eyes and thick black hair, made her appear quite formidable. She possessed an accusatory look that compelled me to confess anything and everything—no matter how innocent—to her instantly. Now, however, she appeared slightly stooped, and her eyes held a reservoir of tears that looked ready to burst at any moment.

"Have the police found out anything new?" I asked.

She shook her head. "They talk a good game, but I think they're out of their league on this one."

"What do you mean?"

She shrugged and then reached out and grabbed my hair in a playful manner. "No witnesses; no clues. They don't know what to do." She let go of my hair and allowed her arm to fall on my shoulder.

"Come now, we can't hide up here all day." We walked down the stairs together, her arm guiding me the whole way.

The afternoon went on far too long. People I barely knew gave me hugs and words of advice that I would never remember. After a while, I excused myself and went into the kitchen and grabbed a beer. I walked out the back door and onto the courtyard. It felt good to be by myself. The scent from the orange trees brought back memories of my dad and me running through the groves, my mother yelling at us to be careful, but still laughing the whole time.

I sat in a wooden chair by the stone fountain, listening to the water as it fell. I took a deep breath and noticed that I was covered in shadow. I turned, and a large man wearing a cowboy hat stood behind me, blocking out the light. He moved toward me, leaving me to stare directly into the sun. I shut my eyes, but black dots popped and bounced off my eyelids. Archibald Roth stood over me. He smelled like a stale cigar. Roth had done a lot of business with my father, turning the rolling hillsides of Orange County into housing developments and shopping centers. I blinked a few times, trying to get my sight back, while he lit up a fresh cigar.

His eyes were like those of a shark—empty, dark, and deadly. I don't know why my dad had liked doing business with him. He'd just say that Archibald Roth was the kind of man who got things done. Whenever I was in his presence, I found a reason to leave; he was no one I wanted to be near. A primal instinct seemed to come alive inside of me whenever he was around, urging me to flee. After what I'd been through today, I felt too exhausted to even stand up. I squinted my eyes at him, trying to get him into focus, but his face was lost behind a cloud of smoke.

"Sorry about your father, Liam."

"Thanks."

"Felix was a helluva man."

The smoke cleared. Roth focused his eyes on his cigar, as if by sheer force he could change it into something else.

"You going to take over the old man's business?"

"Dad asked, but it's really not my thing. But I don't know."

Roth nodded his head, his eyes still on his cigar.

"But you like all that money he gives you, huh? You got your old man's grit. Anyone can see that, even if you can't. You know, Liam, you ought to think about it. I think we could do business together. I think we could make some serious money."

"More than what you already have?"

"Oh hell yeah."

He turned his head from the cigar to me. His eyes still had that focus, and I wondered what he wanted to change me into. I turned away from his stare. Had my father really wanted me in his business, or had he just wanted me to grow up? I didn't know the details of my father's work, but I knew that he'd relied on Marie quite a bit.

"I don't know much about business."

Roth licked his lips and cast his eyes directly into the sun; he didn't even blink. After a moment, he went back to staring at his cigar.

"Well, let's see," he said. "There's Marie. She's tough and she's got that killer instinct. But still she is a woman. This kind of work doesn't wear well on them. She's going to get married and have kids someday." He turned his hollow eyes to me. "And what about your cousin, Carlos?" When I didn't respond, he just laughed. "He's just a farm worker who thinks he's something more. Lazy wetback. Your dad, though, he was one of a kind.

You ready to take control? A son is supposed to follow in his father's footsteps. Or are you one of them hippies?"

Roth's questions were throwing me off. I felt like a child that he wanted to toss into the ocean just to see if I could swim.

"I don't know, okay. My father just died. It's a little early to be talking about this."

Roth laughed. "Boy, you don't know shit, do you? Yes, son, your daddy's dead. The vultures are circling, and y'all better realize it. Predators don't know nothin' about a mourning period."

Instinctively, I turned my eyes upward, but nothing circled overhead. The sky was vacant and lifeless. I heard Roth laugh, and I turned toward him. But he was no longer there. All that remained was the heavy scent of his cigar.

Even though Roth was no longer near me, I had the urge to distance myself from him and our conversation. I got up and walked through the orange groves until I could no longer see the house. I felt safe under the blanket of the fruit trees. I reached up and picked an orange and held it close to my face, trying to let its sweet scent overtake me. I peeled it open and took a big bite, the juices dripping down my fingers. When I was done, I picked another orange, then another. I couldn't stop; I didn't know why. Eventually I noticed I had collected over three dozen oranges, all scattered around me.

Growing up, my mother scolded us about leaving food to waste, so I walked over to one of the sheds to get a basket. As I made my way back to the house, I saw Marie. She stood alone on one of the balconies, staring out to the sea. The sun beamed on her face, yet she appeared cold and pale, almost ghostlike. Her hands gripped the iron railing as if letting go would cause her to fall. A figure stood behind her in the doorway. I couldn't make out whether it was a man or woman, but whoever it was, he or she hadn't moved. Marie didn't appear to notice.

Her eyes focused on something on the distant horizon, something that only she could see.

I placed the basket on the kitchen table and went up the back staircase. I walked quietly toward the room where I had seen Marie and the shadowy figure. Marie was still on the balcony, facing the ocean. I peeked inside the other rooms but didn't see a soul, though I caught the lingering odor of a cigar drifting through the hall.

Marie turned to me. A single tear trickled down her cheek. I wanted to reach out and hold her, but her expression told me not to come near.

I walked slowly out of the room, and when I reached the doorway, I looked back to her. Marie stood frozen like a statue. And then a sudden gust of wind rose up and blew her hair back hard, as if every strand were trying to flee from whatever it was she saw.

CHAPTER SIX

ISABELLE ALWAYS DREW a crowd. She had something about her that attracted both men and women. It was nothing she tried to cultivate. It wasn't something she even understood. While Isabelle had a natural charm that put people at ease, she never let anyone get too close. But when they did come, and they always came, she lit up like a movie star gracing the cover of *Look* magazine. Isabelle had a gift most would cherish and hold on to dearly, but to her it only served as a curse. She would try to slip away to a quiet place, but never seemed to find the peace she sought. Occasionally, I would catch her under one of the orange trees reading a book or writing in her diary. She liked old things. Her books were always worn and frayed at the edges. To her, they held much more than the words contained within the covers. Her diaries, as well, were musty and cracked. She'd scour thrift stores for hours to find the right one. She found more comfort with the past than with the present. Her husband, Glenn, served as an aide to the governor, and Isabelle was destined, as she put it, to eternally put on a happy face.

I found her in my father's office going through some of his papers. She sat on the floor, her legs tucked under her. She looked as sad and, interestingly, as calm as I had ever seen her. She turned her eyes to me and smiled.

"I couldn't take it down there," she told me.

"How long have you been here?"

"For a while now, I suppose. But I could only accept so many condolences, so I retreated. Glenn welcomes these situations. It doesn't matter the occasion, he loves to work a room." Isabelle glanced down at the papers. "Mom seems good, and Marie, well, she's Marie. What about you, Liam? How are you doing?"

I leaned against the wall and sighed. "I don't know what the hell I'm supposed to do. Shake hands, cry, laugh about the good old days. It's going to be different without him. I already miss him."

"I'm sorry," she whispered, though not to me—seemingly to some other unseen person in the room.

She reached out and took my hand, giving it a soft squeeze, and gently pulled me down next to her. "Look at this."

It was an article I had written for *Surf's Up!* magazine.

"He kept them all, you know."

"I didn't even keep all of them," I said. I didn't know why he saved the stories, but it made me feel good knowing that he collected them.

Isabelle smiled at me. "And this," she said.

She held a picture of our mom and dad on their wedding day. Over time the picture must have faded, as the two of them were lost in varying shades of gray. While neither smiled, you could sense a combination of both pride and wedding day jitters.

"Jesus, Mom was stunning," I said.

"When I was little, I asked her what her wedding day was like, and she'd always mention the scent of jasmine surrounding them as they walked down the aisle." Isabelle put the picture down and peered out the door as if she expected someone to walk in.

"Did you ever wonder, Liam, why there's no jasmine growing at the house?"

I shook my head.

"You don't think about these things, do you?"

"I guess not."

"Good for you, Liam." Isabelle nodded at the door and stood up. "I think I need to make another appearance downstairs." She put her hand on my shoulder for just a brief moment before she walked out. As she left the room, I could see the light return to her face as she prepared herself for all the unwanted attention that would surely come her way.

I tried to imagine my parents then. A poor Irish immigrant working as a grocery clerk marries a wealthy American of Mexican descent. They told it the same way every time, with little change.

They met at The Pike amusement park in Long Beach in 1934. My mother had taken the Red Car for a day at the beach. She waited for her friends to get off the Jack Rabbit Racer Roller Coaster, as she had no intention of getting on that wooden contraption, parts of which extended well off the shore and perilously over the water. She didn't like speed, couldn't swim, and questioned the quality of the construction.

My father was standing in line for the roller coaster when he first saw her. She had thick black hair, and her eyes were a shade of blue he had never seen before. He told us that he never had a problem introducing himself to women, but he held back from approaching Mom. Even though she seemed timid and out of place, he had a sense that this woman would not tolerate nonsense of any kind.

"I was nervous," my father said. "I walked up to her for no other reason than I could not imagine passing up such an opportunity."

He introduced himself, but my mother gave him a quick, dismissive glance. Still, she felt herself blush. "I loved the sound of his voice," she said. "So precise and clear, as if he had practiced each word over and over until he got each one just right."

But he was a Mexican, and she had been advised that you had to be careful around them.

He asked her if she'd like to go on the ride with him. She didn't know why she said yes, but the roller coaster just didn't scare her anymore. She said he was awfully dashing in an Errol Flynn sort of way.

My father was taken away by her accent and asked if she were English. "I thought she was going to take my head off," he said.

But she only gave him the raised eyebrow. "I'm Irish, of course, is that a problem for you?"

Six months later they were married and stayed together thirty-two years—until his killer made them part.

CHAPTER SEVEN

THREE DAYS LATER, the morning of the funeral, I was back in the water and on my board. It was a grim, overcast day, and the waves had turned into mush. There had been a couple of sets earlier that produced barely rideable waves, but nothing since. It promised to be a good swell, but the onshore winds had picked up and had blown out the waves. I sensed this lull was going to last a long while. I felt wiped out from the previous night's vigil. My mother had kept us at the church all night, praying. I'd recited the Our Fathers and Hail Marys, but they didn't help. I'd asked God for guidance, though experience taught me not to expect much from him. I had hoped that surfing would give me a brief moment to forget the world, but the lack of sun and the onshore winds made being out on the water miserable. My buddies, Lonnie Reaves and Hike Harkins, were cursing their own gods and debating where the waves might be decent.

"I heard the waves on the North Shore are starting to get pretty bitchin'," Lonnie said. "We should move to the islands. Fuck this shit."

"Man, I'm talking about today. What are we gonna do today?" Hike asked.

These were the days we dreaded. There would be phone calls to friends in Malibu and San Onofre and anywhere up and down the coast, listening to the surf reports on KRLA and KHJ, and then, finally, cruising the coast because somewhere there had to be good waves. It was an optimistic point of view and, I had to admit, searching for waves was better than throwing in the towel, because you'd only drive yourself crazy staying home wondering. You didn't want to learn that there were five-foot waves breaking like a dream at Rincon while you sat on your ass whining like a baby. But the funeral was in a few hours, and I doubted that anything could have improved my mood.

Lonnie gazed out toward the horizon. "The perfect swell's out there, man. One day we'll find it and ride its waves across the whole Pacific, from island to island until we hit the mainland."

Lonnie referred to it as the never-ending swell. Even when it crashed on its final shore, it never really ended. Like Jesus, he said, it would rise again and keep going, forever and ever.

Hike shook his head. "You're talking about riding the same swell for thousands of miles. It's impossible."

"Of course it is. That's why I want to do it."

I paddled back to shore, leaving Lonnie and Hike to debate the existential realities of the never-ending swell. I sat in the sand for a while, staring at the pier and trying not to imagine my father being stabbed. Then I felt a hand tap my shoulder. Dane Lohan stood over me. He wore his standard brown suit. The wind pushed back his sport coat to reveal his gun, nestled in its holster. I gave him a nod, but he wasn't looking at me. His eyes followed a pretty blonde as she glided along the beach.

"We got him, Liam."

I stood up. "What do you mean?"

"We got him. Edward Capuano."

"Eddie? He couldn't hurt a fly."

"He had your father's wallet."

"Why would Eddie—"

"Money, Liam. These types of crimes are always about money."

"Yeah, but Eddie? He doesn't seem like he could kill anyone."

"They never do, Liam. It's always a surprise. And we understand he did have a confrontation with your father at the Beach Club."

"I was there. He wasn't doing anything."

"Maybe so. But junkies need their fix, and he knew your dad had money."

Eddie came from a family of Italian fishermen who lived in San Pedro. Something must have happened to him along the way, and he ended up a bum scraping by in La Bolsa, disowned by his family. I thought about what Dane said about killers—I guessed you really never knew. Still, I'd walked by this guy on a daily basis, giving him spare change when I had it. He had always been so respectful. He'd even blessed those who passed him by and who viewed him as if he were a disease that needed to be avoided at all costs. I couldn't imagine anything that would have set Eddie off against my father. It couldn't have been what had happened at the club.

"I want to see him."

"You do, huh?"

"Yeah."

Dane removed his sunglasses and blew a trace of sand off one of the lenses. "It's probably not a good idea, but we'll see. Anyway, I thought you'd want to know." He put his sunglasses back on, took a last look at the blonde, and then walked back toward the parking lot.

I sat on the sand wondering why I didn't want to tear Eddie to pieces and why I didn't feel better about the police catching the man who had killed my father. I knew the answer of course. Eddie Capuano didn't have it in him to take anyone's life. I needed to talk to him. I needed to know the truth. If my hunch turned out to be right, then Eddie didn't murder him, which meant someone else did. And I had no clue as to who would ever want to murder my father.

CHAPTER EIGHT

THE SCENT OF incense filled the church as if the Holy Spirit itself floated above us. My mother held my hand tightly, keeping me close, keeping me from slipping away to a dark place where she would never be able to find me. I felt uncomfortable in my brand new navy blue suit. I had ignored my father's numerous requests to purchase a good suit, and the one time I finally did get around to buying one was for his funeral. What a son.

The priest talked about the souls of the Just being held in the hands of God. My mother's eyes studied Father Wallace as if he alone could provide answers, as if he could explain the unexplainable. When my mother heard about Eddie Capuano being arrested, she only nodded her head and made the sign of the cross. I was surprised to see no hint of hate or anger in her. Marie sat on the other side of my mom, jaws clenched, her eyes focused on the crucified Jesus. Glenn had his arm around Isabelle, who appeared radiant as always. Each tear that fell from her eyes looked as if it had been painted by a Renaissance artist.

I examined the faces in the church and realized how few of them I recognized. I knew so little of my father's business, and frankly, I liked it that way. He'd been so very proud of what he had built, and that he was able provide so much for his family. Despite the occasional lecture, he'd let me do my own thing, and I'd taken full advantage of it. He'd worked so hard, and I'd lived off his good graces. As my eyes went down the rows of pews, I saw Dawn and her new boyfriend. She whispered something into his ear that caused him to flinch. He gazed at me for a moment, as if by accident, but I knew he wanted to size up his girlfriend's former love. I glanced back to Dawn, and this time she caught my eye. She tilted her head ever so slightly and mouthed, "I'm so sorry," to me. Then she closed her eyes for a second, as if trying to capture in her mind something she felt she might forget.

"We belong neither to darkness nor to night," Father Wallace said.

Dawn's light brown hair barely touched her shoulders, and I saw that she wore the earrings I'd bought her during a long summer weekend we spent together in Rosarito.

Dawn and I were celebrating her graduation from Reed College. We were in Baja, having dinner in the courtyard of our favorite cantina in Rosarito Beach. Tiny bulbs were strung above the dining area like Christmas lights. The glow of her face from the candlelight made her look vulnerable, but more beautiful than I could imagine. This was her. No makeup, the scent of the ocean in her hair, her brown eyes that always saw more of me than I was willing to give.

"I know what you're thinking," she said.

"No, you don't."

"Yes, I do. You can't wait for dinner to end so we can get in the ocean again. Look, you're blushing."

She was right. I couldn't wait for our late-night ritual for the weekend. We'd find a deserted stretch of beach, take off our clothes, and wade into the warm waters of Baja beneath a crescent moon. We'd dive under the waves and come up together in each other's arms. Dawn would wrap herself around me like she never wanted to let go; and we'd go under again, and she'd push me away, daring me to chase her. I loved how she glided through the water, the way her body moved, sensual and pure. She was one with the ocean. We joked that in a previous life she must have been a dolphin. I'd ask her what I might have been in a previous life.

"Nothing," she said. "This is your first life, your first time here, and I'm your teacher. It's up to me to show you what life and love is all about."

Dawn leaned over our little wooden table and kissed me softly on the lips, as a mariachi band serenaded the couple next to us.

"What was that for?" I asked.

She raised her eyebrows and gave me a funny look. "I love you, Liam."

Whenever she said those words, I felt undeserving of her love. Dawn found that part of me that I was frightened to know existed. A place I didn't like to visit and tried to stay away from and ignore. A secret place where I hid my weaknesses, doubts, and fears. A place that Dawn knew about and yet, somehow, still loved me.

"I love you, too." I repeated those words to her countless times, and each time I uttered them, I felt exposed. I did love her, but the vulnerability those words revealed never failed to overwhelm me.

She reached out and held my hands. Suddenly awkward, Dawn seemed unable to look me in the eye.

"I have something that I need to tell you," she said.

"Tell me."

"You're the one for me, Liam. I've always known it. You're the one. You need to know that. But I think, I think I might be pregnant." Then her eyes found mine and I had to look away. It felt like Muhammad Ali had punched me in the chest. My stomach dropped, and I heard a gasp come from somewhere deep inside of me. I wanted to escape. I wanted to be somewhere else. It didn't matter where—just anywhere but here.

"What's wrong?" she asked. Her voice sounded small and on the verge of breaking. "What is it?"

I couldn't respond. I didn't know how to respond. Dawn pulled her hands from me. I tried to hold on, to keep them next to me, but my palms were damp and cold and her fingers slipped away.

The priest's voice broke through my reverie. "I am the resurrection and the life. Whoever believes in me, even if he dies, will live."

Dawn opened her eyes and focused them on Father Wallace. Her boyfriend caught me staring at her. This time he gave me a polite, sympathetic nod, acknowledging my grief, and then he put his arm around her. I got his message: *She belongs to me.* He resembled John Sebastian of The Lovin' Spoonful. He had hippie written all over him: bell-bottom pants, long hair, and granny glasses. I didn't expect him to be so different than me and, I thought, so wrong for her.

Dawn taught at an elementary school in Santa Ana. She had always wanted to shape young minds and to inspire people, a talent that came naturally to her. I thought about where we might be if I'd had the courage to respond to what she revealed to me in Rosarito. If only I had stepped up; if only I had been the person she thought I could be.

It wasn't the first time I had painted a picture of our future, a picture that hurt too much to dwell upon: the image of the two of us lying in bed, the morning sunlight dancing on the sheets, a warm ocean breeze blowing through an open window tossing her hair gently over the pillows, and two kids, maybe a son and a daughter, rushing into our room to greet us. But I wasn't part of her future anymore; it belonged to him now. And I couldn't do a thing about it.

Dawn didn't stay for the burial. I wished I could have passed on it, too. I don't recall what was said or how long we were there. I stared at the hole where my father's body would forever lie, alone and cold under a green, manicured lawn. Life would go on without him, and after a while he would just be a memory. Walking back to the car, I knew I had to leave him behind, and that whatever happened in the future, he wouldn't be a part of it. Though my mother told us we would always carry him with us, I wondered if that were true. "Good-bye, Dad," I whispered. I closed my eyes and placed my hand to my heart. I glanced back at his casket as it sat alone in the middle of the cemetery. The workers respectfully waited nearby, waiting to lower him down to his final resting place and cover him with dirt. The limousine driver stood waiting for me, ready to escort me into a new world.

Before stepping into the limo, I noticed three figures standing in the shadow of a distant oak tree. Noriko Kiyan and her daughters, Bonnie and Joy, were dressed in black, their heads bowed. I hadn't noticed them before, and I thought for a moment they were attending someone else's funeral. Bonnie was my age, and we had gone to La Bolsa High together. But I didn't know much about her other than that she was an honor student and that she kept to herself. The Kiyans were very private. Occasionally, you'd see them around town shopping, except for Joy, who they kept hidden away as if she were a delicate artifact that might break if exposed to the world at large.

I watched as they approached my father's casket, their steps small and cautious. Mrs. Kiyan held Joy's hand. When she reached for Bonnie's hand, Bonnie refused to take it. They stopped at the site, and the three put their heads down in a silent prayer. I had no idea where they knew my father from. I wondered, too, why they waited for everyone to leave before they paid their respects. As the limo pulled away, I glanced out the car window and saw the Kiyans knelt in prayer. Bonnie lifted her head and watched as we drove away. I turned to my mother, her eyes focusing on nothing, her hands clutching her rosary so hard I thought the beads would break loose. Marie glared back at the Kiyans, her eyes as cold as death.

CHAPTER NINE

I WOKE UP WITH a hangover. My brain felt like hundreds of surfboards were crashing against my skull. Hike and Lonnie had taken me to The Belly of the Whale bar, and each beer had tasted better than the last. I'd thought the alcohol would take away the pain and help me ease back into the world. By night's end, though, I'd felt more depressed than before.

I hadn't been able to sleep. My bed had twirled like the teacup ride at Disneyland. Between the spinning and the nausea, visions of Eddie Capuano on the pier the night my father died had drifted in and out of my mind, like a dream that refused to take hold. I couldn't imagine what would drive Eddie to stick a knife into my father's back. Eddie Capuano was no killer, but I remembered what my old psychology professor had once said: that under the right circumstances, any one of us is capable of anything, including murder.

I crawled out of bed shortly after sunrise and made my way to the bathroom where I popped a couple of aspirins. I made some instant coffee and walked out to my front porch. Across the way from me on Golden Sun sat a large oil field and behind my house, separated by a chain-link fence, stood the back lot of a nursery where dozens of potted palm trees had been arranged, giving it a slight island feel. Normally I welcomed the isolation, but today it only unsettled me. I took a seat on the lawn chair and watched the tide roll in as gray clouds sat low over the ocean. I couldn't hear a thing, not the oil wells or the ocean. I could see life and movement around me, but still not a sound. A '65 Mustang raced by on PCH, but the expected engine noise didn't accompany it. It felt like the fog had crept into my ears and blocked out all the sounds. The silence was overwhelming. I held my coffee cup with both hands and wondered if this was how death would be: silence and an eternal grayness that wiped the color from everything. I took a sip of coffee and thought about taking some more aspirin. Then the phone rang, breaking the silent wall that had surrounded me. It was Hike.

"Hey man, the waves are shit here, but Slow Joe called me and said they're breaking chest-high at Trestles."

I pulled the phone away from my ear for a second, but the only thing I heard was Hike humming a song that I recognized, but couldn't quite place.

"I'll pass this time."

"Waves, man. Riding them is the answer to life's hangovers." Hike, no matter how much he drank, never felt the effects of a hangover.

"There're some things I have to take care of today."

"Okay, man. We'll catch you next time."

"Yeah, next time."

I hung up the phone and dialed Dane at the police station.

"I want to see him," I said.

Dane wasn't eager for me to see Eddie Capuano.

"I don't think it's a good idea."

"I'm not going to do anything to him. I just want to talk to him."

"He's in pretty bad shape. He's begging for a fix. I think he was doing a lot more than just drinking lately. We've been seeing a lot more of that. I don't get it."

I knew what he meant. I was seeing it, too.

"Anyway, we're shipping him over to County tomorrow."

"I'm coming over now. Dane, please, I just need to see him."

"It's not a good idea, but I might grant you a few minutes. We'll have a guard with you at all times, just in case."

I put the phone down and wondered what the hell I thought I was trying to accomplish.

They put me in a small room that reeked of cigarettes. The walls, once white, were now a tobacco-stained version of beige, and peeling, like open sores. A chipped Formica table and four chairs stood in the middle of the room. I sat in one of the chairs that faced the door. I didn't know what to say to Eddie. I couldn't really say why I was there, but something didn't feel right. My father had always advised me not to act on emotions, but to examine the facts first. All I knew was that Eddie had been found with my father's wallet, but that didn't mean he had killed him.

The door opened and a guard who looked as if he had wrestled Freddie Blassie one too many times pushed Eddie into the room.

Eddie Capuano was cuffed and scared. He fell into the seat across the table from me.

"Five minutes," the guard said. He stood by the door, arms folded over his chest.

"Hey, Liam. Thanks for coming." Eddie said it as though I were visiting him at his home on a Sunday afternoon. His eyes, though, were red, and he kept glancing to his side as if some menacing figure hovered next to him. He bit his fingernails like they were licorice, and his legs bounced in a rhythm that was impossible to keep time with.

"Hello, Eddie."

"What's up, Liam?"

I turned to the guard. "Does he even know why he's in jail?"

"You have four minutes."

"Four? You can't round up back to five?"

I caught the trace of a smirk on the guard's face as he shook his head.

"Eddie, do you know why you're here?"

He looked at me, confused.

"Cuz you wanted to see me?"

"No. Do you know why you're in jail?"

"They said I killed somebody."

"They said you killed my dad, Eddie. My father."

"Felix? Mr. Sol?" He closed his eyes as if trying to recall something. "I saw him. He was on the pier. He gave me five dollars."

"What?"

"It was foggy, man. And I hurt real bad, just like now. They won't give me cigarettes. Everyone here's smoking and the guards won't even let me bum one stinking cigarette."

"You saw him on the pier?"

"Yes. He gave me the money, and he told me to go away, which was what I was going to do anyway, cuz what I needed wasn't on the pier."

He continued to gnaw on his fingernails; a small trickle of blood slid down his index finger. I turned back to the guard again, and he shook his head like Eddie Capuano wouldn't know the truth if it hit him in the face.

"How did you get his wallet?"

"I don't know. I didn't know I had it."

"Okay, time's up." The guard walked over and pulled Eddie Capuano's chair away from the table.

"I wasn't the only one on the pier."

"Now," the guard said. He lifted Eddie Capuano as if he weighed all of five ounces.

"What? Do you know who it was?"

"It was foggy, man, real foggy. Can you make sure these guys give me some smokes? I could use one, Liam."

"Who else was on the pier?"

"Time's up," the guard said.

"Eddie, who was it?"

"I don't know, man. I don't."

The guard grabbed Eddie by the shoulder and hauled him out of the room. I stayed in the chair and wondered who Eddie Capuano had seen on the pier.

CHAPTER TEN

That night, I attended a small party on the beach. We staked our place on the north side of the pier so we'd attract less attention from both the police and the tourists. I made sure to sit where I wouldn't have a view of the pier.

We had a fire going, and bottles of wine were passed around along with a few joints. I didn't know why I'd decided to attend the party. I was a fool to think this could cheer me up, or even for a moment help me forget. People talked all around me, but I didn't understand a word they said; they might as well have been speaking in tongues. I couldn't shake the image of my father on the pier, completely unaware that it was to be his last night on earth. I continued to have serious doubts that Eddie Capuano had killed him, yet Dane seemed so sure they had arrested the right man. I recalled Eddie's behavior when I'd seen him in jail. His hands shook too much to hold a knife, let alone stab someone. And had he really seen anyone else on the pier? God, I didn't know what to think.

A couple of guys pulled out their guitars and strummed "Sittin' on a Fence." Hike, who had a pretty decent voice, tried to imitate Mick Jagger, but failed miserably.

"It must be his lips, man," he said. "I can't do it."

"He's so ugly," a girl I'd never seen before said in a voice that sounded like a wasted Minnie Mouse. Lonnie had his arm around her, hoping for a nice finish to his night. "I mean, u-g-l-y," she said. I glanced at Lonnie. He smiled and shrugged, as if to acknowledge that his sacrifice would soon pay off. The image of him with that girl reminded me of me, or more precisely, of the person I'd been only a few short days ago—and I didn't like what I saw.

"I think he's damn sexy."

The voice belonged to Raven Andrews, her red hair glowing like wild flames in the light of the campfire. She caught my eye and gave me a wink. Raven and I had a strange relationship. There were times when she would knock on my door at two in the morning and want to talk all night about whatever she was obsessed with at the moment. Sometimes it would lead us into the bedroom, and sometimes I'd end up sitting with her as she cried endlessly for no apparent reason. Raven lived in a different world than most of us. She loved to watch us surf, but never did she put even her toe into the water. Raven had the IQ of a rocket scientist, yet you'd see her holding up the line at the A&W trying in vain to decide between a Mama Burger and a Papa Burger. She would disappear for days on end, her family never knowing where she had run off to. She must have recently returned from one of those absences, because I hadn't seen her in a while.

Raven came over and sat next to me and put her hand to my cheek.

"I heard about your father. I'm really sorry, Liam."

Not knowing how to respond, I just nodded my head.

"I haven't seen you for a while, Raven."

"Been up to Big Sur. Monterey, Frisco, here, there, and everywhere."

She squeezed in close to me. She smelled like cinnamon, and I suddenly realized how lonely I felt. I caught her eyes, and she gave me that smile, letting me know I had the green light.

"I missed you," she whispered.

Raven wasn't one to be seduced. She took the lead and never worried what others thought or said. She nuzzled closer, her lips grazing my ear, her hand resting on my thigh. At any other time her attention would have been welcomed, but it just made me feel lonelier. I knew that if I went off with her, it would only make the sadness that had enveloped me stronger. Yet I wanted to be with her. She grabbed my hand and helped me to my feet. She led me away from the fire and in the direction of my house. As we approached the path to the cliff, I stopped.

"What?" Raven asked.

I didn't know how to answer her question. I didn't want to be alone. I wanted to be with her. I wanted what she offered, but I couldn't do it. She saw it in my eyes.

Raven let go of my hand and playfully kicked a little sand on my feet. "Hang in there, Liam, okay?"

"Yeah." My voice cracked in the night air.

She narrowed her eyes, nodded her head slightly, and walked back to the party. The bonfire burned strong, the embers floating in the air like failed fireworks. I walked up the path alone. When I made it to the top, I couldn't help but look out at the pier. And the question came to me: what was my father doing on the pier that night?

CHAPTER ELEVEN

THE PALE-FACED MAN

THE PALE-FACED MAN stood in the hall, just a few feet from the open cell door. It was the only cell holding a prisoner. He heard the guards teasing Eddie Capuano.

“Here, little rats, go to Eddie’s cell. He wants visitors.” The guard taunting him was short and muscular, too muscular, as if he spent all of his free time at Muscle Beach. A pussy, in other words.

“No. Keep them away. Please keep them out,” Eddie screamed. He was terrified, as if witnessing a vision of himself burning for eternity. The pale-faced man almost felt sorry for him. The guards were cruel, and they liked having power over the weak. Typical cops.

“They’re crawling on the walls. They’re after me. Stop them. Get them out.” Eddie blubbered like a baby now.

“We can’t help you, Eddie. They’re coming after you, and we can’t stop them, Eddie. They want you,” the taller one said. He clearly hoped for the approval of the shorter, muscular guard. The pale-faced man watched the taller guard’s eyes roam over his partner’s body. The tall guy was a fag, all right. And the shorter guy was a sadistic little shit.

Eddie continued to wail. The guards laughed and slapped their knees like they were watching an Abbott and Costello movie. He wished he could kill the two guards as well, but that would defeat the purpose of his mission.

The pale-faced man stepped into the cell and pounded his fist twice on the wall. The two guards jerked and turned to him. The shorter guard was about to say something, but then froze as if he knew instinctively that he was in the presence of evil. The pale-faced man watched as their faces lost their color. The shorter one nudged the taller one, and the two slouched away, just like they were supposed to do.

The cell smelled like human feces and cold sweat. Eddie lay on his bed as if his body were nailed to the mattress. He suffered from the shakes, and his hands swatted frantically at the rats only he could see.

"No!"

Eddie covered his head with the blanket, his body convulsing.

"Help me," he screamed.

"I'll help you," the pale-faced man said calmly.

Eddie pulled the blanket down until it rested just under his chin. He resembled a small, frightened child, hiding from the monsters that lurked beneath his bed.

"You will?"

The pale-faced man examined Eddie's face. The bags that nested under his eyes made it appear as if he'd been on the wrong end of a fistfight. He knew they weren't from a fight, though. Eddie had junkie eyes. Beads of sweat ran down Eddie's hairline and dripped from his chin. His breath reeked as if his insides were rotting away.

"Close your eyes," the pale-faced man said.

"No, no. You're here to hurt me. What's wrong with your eyes? What are you?"

"I'm here to take your pain from you."

"And the rats?"

"I'm taking them away, too. Now, be a good boy and do as I say."

Eddie closed his eyes and tried to take a deep breath, but he gagged as if he were choking on his own saliva.

The pale-faced man put his hand over Eddie's mouth while his other hand pinched Eddie's nose shut. He pressed down hard on Eddie's mouth. He could have suffocated him with a pillow, but he preferred to watch them die. Each one gave him the same look: shock, fear, panic, and finally, resignation. He wanted them to see him as well. The pale-faced man liked knowing that he would be the last person his victims would ever see, for now and on to eternity.

Eddie's eyes opened wide, like a bug. Eddie, as predicted, went through the looks, but when panic struck, he started to struggle, his arms trying to grab at the pale-faced man's face. The pale-faced man liked it when they tried to resist. He liked identifying the very moment where they lost their will to live. As with others, Eddie's resolve didn't last. Tears welled up in Eddie's eyes, and then the pale-faced man pressed down harder until Eddie started to slip into unconsciousness. And then he sang Eddie a lullaby. "Row, row, row your boat, gently down the stream." By the time he got to "life is but a dream," Eddie was dead.

The pale-faced man ripped up the bed sheet and made a crude noose. He tied it securely around the top bar. Then he picked up Eddie, surprised by how light he was. He put the noose around Eddie's neck and let him fall. The neck snapped like a toothpick.

It wasn't his best work, but it didn't need to be. This was going to be read as a suicide. No one would examine the death scene very closely. Not that it mattered. The pale-faced man knew he would never be caught. He could turn into a ghost whenever he desired.

But he wasn't supposed to disappear just yet. He needed to hang around in case anyone started asking more questions. He hoped for the worst possible outcome. He hoped they'd ask him to kill again.

CHAPTER TWELVE

MARIE CALLED ME with the news. Dane Lohan had made a special trip to the house to let her know. I wondered when he was going to make his move on Marie. I kind of wished I could be there when it happened, so I could see the results.

"It doesn't make sense, Marie."

"He was crazy, Liam. He killed Felix and then killed himself."

"What did Mom say?"

"What do you want her to say?" She paused for a moment and then let out a sigh. "She and Isabelle went to church to pray for him. Can you believe that? Felix gets killed, and now they're praying for the soul of the man who killed him."

"Something's wrong. I don't think Eddie had the strength or the will to stick a knife into anyone."

"Liam, let it go. Just let it go. Let Brona grieve in peace."

"Marie—"

"Let it die, Liam. Christ, now you want to be involved in the family? What, the waves aren't breaking right today? Just do what you've always done. We'll handle everything."

"Marie, don't you wonder why Dad was on the pier?"

"Good-bye, Liam."

That night I went to Rosa's Mexican Restaurant. It sat across from the ocean on PCH, about a mile north of the pier, with a clear view of the ocean. Rosa's was a good place to hang out with friends, though it was a bit of a dive. The jukebox played Mexican songs, and the tacos had a bite to them rarely found north of the border. The night was warm, and the place was packed with surfers and other locals. A few people stopped by to pay their respects.

Bobby Dix sat at the bar. He had the tough-guy stare-down perfected, as if he'd seen *The Wild One* once too often. I'd only seen him at Rosa's a few times. Dix usually hung out at the biker bars on PCH. Dix was not a good guy. He and his friends liked to kick the shit out of any kook who dropped in on his wave, or anyone who dared touch what he referred to as his waters. If it was your wave and he dropped in on you, which he tended to do, you just kept your mouth shut unless you wanted your face bashed in. When the Watts Riots were going on, he and his friends drove to L.A. to watch the destruction of the city and to cheer on cops who were beating down on the Negroes. They loved watching the City of Angels burn. Still, while he terrorized most everybody, for reasons I never understood, he never cut me off in the waves and never gave me shit of any kind. Dix was talking to a very pale man who was puffing intensely on a cigarette.

Hike and Lonnie were determined to get me out of my funk. We had just toasted the sunset, holding our beers up high in salute. The two of them had been trying to talk me into a trip down to Baja, which, they promised, would be the cure for everyone. They'd been a little testy lately as the strong onshore winds continued to kill a good southern swell.

"Liam, let's get you away from La Bolsa," Lonnie said. "We'll get you across the border and back on the board. Find some *senoritas* and you can rediscover all that's right with the world."

"I don't know, guys. The water isn't exactly a place of comfort for me these days."

"Everything's different in Baja, Liam."

"You think so?"

"Liam," Hike pleaded. "We gotta go to Baja. I can't take this, man. We have to go."

It would have been a perfect time to leave. Just get out of Dodge and let everything work itself out. No one needed me here. Come back in a week or two and get on with my life. Yet, for some reason I couldn't identify, I didn't want to go.

"What would your dad want?" Lonnie asked.

"He'd want me to quit surfing and to get on with my life."

Hike took a swat at Lonnie. "Stupid question, ass-wipe. No. He'd want you to be happy, Liam."

I shrugged and took a sip of my beer. I could see my mood brought Hike and Lonnie down. They were doing their best to shake me from my funk, but I was at a loss as to how to help them.

I glanced over at Bobby Dix, who gave me a nod before turning back to the bar. The guy with the pale face put his arm around Dix and whispered something to him. Dix turned away with a grimace, as if he'd just received some terrible news. He tried to regain himself, and then he walked slowly out of the restaurant. The guy turned and gave me a long look before going back to his drink. He had black hair combed straight back, in stark contrast to his very white face. His eyes were dark and moist like wet tar.

"So, what's the story with Raven? No way you turned her down. She is the perfect fuck, I bet. No guilt. No dinner and a movie. She might even be better than the perfect wave." Hike leaned close to me. "She doesn't like anybody else. She digs you, man. She comes back to the party and she's not letting any guy get close to her."

"Hike's right. I don't know what she sees in you, but I wish she saw that in me. She's a very spiritual girl. I think we'd connect."

I looked at him. "Spiritual?"

"Sometimes it's not about sex, it's about soul," Lonnie said with a wink.

A hot blast of wind came up, blowing hard through the window screens, tossing napkins off the tables. It howled as if it came not from the air, but from some horrible place below the earth. The restaurant went silent as the first gusts of the Santa Anas of the season arrived.

"There is a God," Hike yelled. "They're early this year. Out of sight."

The Santa Anas are hot and dry and whip downward from the northeast. They begin to kick up dust in the Great Basin and blow past the lost graves of Indian warriors and white settlers. They scream over the Mojave Desert, past the remains of the Dust Bowl immigrants whose dreams died along with their cars on the road to paradise. The winds continue to collect speed and power and heat as they howl through the passes and canyons of the San Gabriels, all the way to the coast, crashing into Catalina Island, until they die somewhere over the Pacific. Depending on where you lived, they were either a curse or a blessing. They cleared out the smog from the valleys and made picture-postcard days across the basin, but they also brought destruction and sleepless nights. They could hold up waves like a wet dream, yet they made for dangerous fire conditions in the hillsides and in the mountains. They were said to bring out the earthquakes and the crazies. And right now I felt the winds creep into my chest and make me think about things I didn't want to think about. Suddenly, everything felt wrong—nothing I could put my finger on, but I had to get up. I had to move. I had to get out of the restaurant. I rose up from the table as if picked up by the wind.

"I've got some stuff to do."

"Where are you going?"

I walked out of the restaurant, leaving them without a response. A Spanish love song played on the jukebox, the tune following me like a forgotten friend. I only understood a few of the words, but I could tell the singer's heart had been broken and she wasn't sure if it would ever mend. The Santa Anas blew hot and hard on my face. I stood still for a moment, listening to the music and the laughter that drifted through the open windows of the restaurant. I could see my friends, but I felt like I lived on a different planet, one where I was the outsider. One of the things that kept coming back to me, the thing I didn't want to face, was what one of the cops asked down at the beach when they found my dad.

Just how well did he know his father?

It wasn't his words as much as his tone, like it shouldn't have come as such a great surprise to me that my dad had been murdered. Then there was Marie's attitude, Noriko, Bonnie, and Joy Kiyan showing up at the cemetery, my dad on the pier alone so late at night, and Eddie Capuano's suicide. All of these might be easily explained, but I knew I couldn't leave until I found the answers. Something deep inside held me and wasn't going to let me free until I knew more. I couldn't erase the feeling that Eddie Capuano had died an innocent man and that my father's killer was free, and getting the last laugh on all of us.

I went out to the parking lot, where I saw the pale-faced guy walking away from my truck. I stopped and felt my hands ball into fists. As he passed me, he whispered something I didn't understand.

"What?" I asked.

The pale-faced man didn't respond, but kept walking until he got to the front door of Rosa's, where he stopped and gave me a lopsided grin before stepping inside. In his wake I caught the overwhelming scent of something that smelled like cloves. Another big gust of wind came up, and I felt the hairs on the back of my neck rise, as if the Devil Winds were trying to tell me to leave well enough alone.

CHAPTER THIRTEEN

EARLY THE NEXT morning I drove down PCH toward my parents' house. The winds were still coming on hard and had cleared out both the fog and smog, leaving a glorious day in their wake. I could see the San Gabriel Mountains to my left and Catalina Island to my right. I gazed out at the waves, wondering how many people had called in sick today. Days this pretty didn't come along that often, and I wondered how long this swell was going to last. Still, Hike's theory about bad things happening on beautiful days echoed in my mind.

As I drove through the intersection of Ocean Boulevard and PCH, Dave Hull, the Hullabalooer, screamed about all the happenings on the Sunset Strip. I turned the dial to KHJ, then to KFWB, but found nothing but commercials. I turned the radio off and rolled down the window to let the warm air flow inside. Up ahead I saw one of the Kiyan Fruit stands that seemed to be on every major street in La Bolsa. The Kiyans' farm was just off Santa Anita Canyon road. They owned over one hundred acres and grew mostly strawberries. They were very private people, and I couldn't imagine what they had to do with my father.

Though my parents' house wasn't far from the beach, it always felt at least ten degrees hotter. I looked out beyond the orange groves to the dry brush, and I knew, with the aid of the Santa Anas, just one match could take all this away in a few short minutes. I got out of my truck and watched the palm trees that surrounded the house bend in the wind like they were following an exercise routine led by Jack LaLanne.

Inside the house, maids I'd never seen before bustled about, cleaning everything in sight. The thick adobe walls, along with the ceiling fans, kept the house cool, but the air was filled with the scent of Windex and Pledge. Tree branches banged up against the side of the house like burglars trying to break in. The winds usually died down by late morning and didn't pick up again until the evening, but I had a feeling they were going to stay strong all day.

Our maid, Graciella, greeted me. She was only five feet tall, but she was a strong thing. I'd seen her pick up heavy pieces of furniture that would take two professional movers to carry. She had been working for my parents since before I was born. Graciella had two sons, both of whom were in the Marines and stationed in Vietnam. I'd never met them. She told me once that she didn't like bringing her kids to work.

"Hello, Mr. Liam. I believe they are in the kitchen eating breakfast. I've prepared some old favorites for you. Would you also like me to make *huevos rancheros* for you?"

I thanked her, told her that I wasn't hungry and, for the umpteenth time, that she didn't have to call me "Mr. Liam." Graciella smiled and turned away and said something in Spanish to one of the maids my mother must have hired for the day. I could only pick up a few words as my father hadn't wanted us to learn the language—a language, he'd told us, that in this country was only for the poor and the ignorant.

Isabelle sat alone in the kitchen reading the *Herald Examiner*. The *Los Angeles Times*, *The Register*, and the *La Bolsa Tribune* were scattered around her on the table.

"Hey, Isabelle."

I must have surprised her because she flinched, but Isabelle being Isabelle, she carried it off well.

"Good morning, Liam." She rose out of her chair. "Can I get you something to eat?"

"No. Sit down. I'll just have some coffee."

She made a move to the coffee pot, but I beat her to it. I poured myself a cup and sat down across from her. Along with the scent of the coffee, the kitchen smelled of Graciella's "old favorites"—freshly made tortillas, rice, and refried beans. When the three of us were kids, Graciella always had them cooking on the stove, ready for us to eat anytime we desired. I'm surprised none of us turned into Fat Albert.

"Where is everybody?"

"Mom's outside directing the gardeners. She's having them water the grounds, the roof of the house, clearing away brush, you name it. These winds terrify her to no end."

"And Marie?"

Isabelle shrugged as if she couldn't care less. They'd never been that close, but her reaction was so indifferent I wondered if the two of them had exchanged words. They were such opposites. Isabelle was the magnet who attracted people, and Marie, with her force field, kept everyone at bay. They got along, but their relationship seemed stiff and formal, as if they were rivals of some kind. Still, Marie had a protective streak when it came to Isabelle. Isabelle once told me that when they were in high school, Marie threatened to beat up a boy who had called Isabelle a "taco-bending whore." I remember being astonished when Isabelle said that Marie had stood up for her, throwing down the schoolyard declaration of "after school" to him. The boy, much bigger than Marie, tried to laugh it off, but she narrowed her eyes and stepped up to him, inches from his face. She whispered something into his ear that Isabelle couldn't hear. The boy's face turned ashen, as if he'd been visited by a nightmare that had finally come to life.

"I'm sorry," he blurted out. Then he turned to Isabelle and said softly, "I'm sorry. I was just joking around. I didn't mean to hurt your feelings."

The boy made a point of being very polite to her afterward, though he did transfer schools at the end of the semester.

Isabelle always seemed to glide gracefully through life, and I wondered how much Marie had to do with that.

"How is everyone holding up?" I asked.

Isabelle forced a smile. "Mom is keeping quite busy, and Marie, well... she's been busy, too, as you can see."

She slid the front page of the *La Bolsa Tribune* across the table toward me. One of the headlines jumped right out at me.

"Glenn is running for the state Senate?"

Isabelle gazed out the back window. The brush on the hillsides appeared browned and brittle from the long, dry summer.

"Yes, and for this district. We'll be living here at the house for a while until we find our own place."

"What has this got to do with Marie?"

She turned to me, her eyes suddenly dark and lightless.

"Is Gus retiring?" I asked.

State Senator Gus Schilling and my father went back a long way. He and his wife, Ellen, came over to the house often and even took vacations with my mom and dad.

"No. She's going after him." Isabelle started to organize the newspapers into a neat pile.

"Marie hasn't been happy with how Gus has been doing his job, and she knows Glenn has political ambitions. She's been lobbying him to run since Dad died. Of course, it didn't take much to convince Glenn. He's so easily influenced."

I knew that my dad had let Marie get more involved in the company lately, and he'd even proudly commented to me that she had more balls than most men.

"What did Mom say?"

"She doesn't care, Liam. I don't think she was ever that fond of Gus and Ellen."

"Why?"

"I don't know, but Marie and Dad had been arguing about the business lately. I don't think he was pleased with her plans for the city. And Marie thought that Dad wasn't thinking big enough."

Before I could ask, Isabelle told me she didn't know anything more about what led to the disagreements.

I glanced down at my coffee. "The day he died, Dad asked me if I wanted to get involved in the business."

Isabelle closed her eyes. "Yes, I heard that he asked you."

There was an anxiety in her voice, and anger and defensiveness bubbled up inside of me.

"You don't think I could do it?"

"Of course you could, but..." She put her hands on mine and pressed them down on the table. "You can't. Liam, you're the only one, the only one who isn't..." She studied me like I was fragile and breakable.

"The only one who isn't what?" I asked.

"No. Liam." She pushed her hands down harder. They felt cold and clammy. "Don't ask. Don't. You're not Dad. Remember that. You're not him. You're not—"

My mom suddenly marched into the kitchen. "Well, I don't know what else to do. These Devil Winds will be the ruin of us yet."

She never referred to them as the Santa Anas, but always by their nickname. God had nothing to do with them, but surely Satan had his hand in them. She gazed out the window at the winds and the hillsides and shook her head.

"I don't know where Carlos has run off to. He's been completely absent since Felix's death." She turned around and saw me at the table.

"Oh, hello, Liam. I didn't even notice you there. Now, what brings you by? Come and give your mother a hug." I stood up, and she wrapped me in her arms. Again, I noticed a trace of alcohol on her breath. Isabelle started to walk out of the kitchen, then stopped and turned my way. She shook her head, her eyes trying to communicate something to me—but I wasn't sure what—and then left the room.

"Carlos will come around, Mom. He has nowhere else to go," I said.

My mom let go and gave me a long look. "Would you like some breakfast? I can have Graciella make you some of those eggs you like?"

"No. I'm fine."

"Sit down, then."

She let out a heavy sigh as she lowered herself to the chair. "I'm finally getting the house back into shape. I've been letting things go since your father passed."

She put the palm of her hand to her cheek and inspected the hillsides. "I don't know why I didn't have them clear the brush earlier. That fire in Chimney Canyon last year was an evil one." She was referring to the Loop Fire in the Angeles National Forest where thirteen firefighters had lost their lives. Any fire in Southern California, she thought, could, with the aid of the Devil Winds, reach anywhere.

My mom kept talking, but Isabelle's reaction stirred in my mind. Was she trying to protect me from my family? Or could there have been something about my father that she didn't want me to know?

"What's wrong, Liam?"

Mom gave me the look—the raised eyebrows, the knowing smile—the one that always made me reveal anything, it seemed, she wanted from me.

"Mom, what was Dad doing on the pier that night?"

She folded her arms across her chest, her eyes focused on some flaw on the kitchen table. "I was the cause of it. We got into a fight and I wouldn't let up." She placed her hands on her hips. "My temper, you know. It wasn't over much. It's the little things that cause such damage. Anyway, as he always did when we got into a row, he went out. The ocean always had such a calming effect on him, you know."

It's funny what you forget. My parents didn't get into very many arguments, but when they did, it always ended with my dad walking out and my mom crying on the sofa, her sobs passing through the halls and drifting up the stairs and into our beds. The next morning Marie, Isabelle, and I would walk down together, silently dreading what the day might bring, but we'd find them in the kitchen, teasing each other as if nothing had ever happened.

"I shouldn't have let him go."

"It wasn't your fault, Mom."

She reached over and patted my hand. Another blast of wind came up and rattled the windows.

"I best get outside and see what I can do. You'll be staying for lunch, I hope?"

I told her I would. She smiled and walked out the back door, stopping on the patio for a brief second, her eyes once again focused on the hillsides, and I knew she believed they would explode into flames at any moment.

I took a sip of the coffee. It was lukewarm, but still better than the instant I made at my place. My father did have a valid reason to be out on the pier by himself that night. I should have felt better about it, but I couldn't shake the feeling that there was more to my father's death.

I walked upstairs to his office, but stopped just outside the door when I heard Marie talking to someone on the phone.

"I know you're surprised, but you shouldn't be. I was on board with this the whole time."

She paused for a moment.

"Of course, we can meet. Should I bring our next state senator?... The Beach Club. See you then, Archibald."

I walked into the office. Marie was seated at our father's desk, softly humming a Beatles song as she wrote something on a pad of paper.

"Talking to Archibald Roth?"

Marie glanced up and glared at me like I was trespassing.

"Not that it's any of your business, but yes, I was. Things still need to get done, Liam. You do want to continue living rent-free in your little shack, don't you? Well, the business won't run by itself."

I let that pass. Marie could spend all day reminding me what a bum she thought I was.

"Isabelle doesn't seem too thrilled that Glenn is running for office."

She put her pen down and let out a sigh.

"She'll come around." Her voice turned soft. "Isabelle's going to be fine. Sooner or later Glenn was going to run for office, whether I encouraged him or not. It's better that he run down here where he has built-in support."

"Meaning you and Archibald Roth?"

Her eyes narrowed. "Yes, and others. There are a lot of interests involved, Liam."

"Whose interests? Archibald Roth? I don't trust the guy, and you shouldn't either."

Her eyes regarded me like I was a third grader who had just challenged a teacher. "What are you doing? You don't know anything, anything about the business. Dad groomed me to run the company, not you."

"He wanted me to get involved."

She let out a harsh laugh.

"Go to hell, Marie." I felt like pounding her. "You know, I'm sorry you hate me. I don't know what I did that caused you to treat me like shit, Marie, but I'm sick of it."

She shot out of her chair, and then she stood still for a second before walking slowly toward me. Her hands were balled up into fists, and her jaw was clenched tight. I felt sure she was going to take a swing at me.

"Don't for a second think I don't love you, Liam." Her tone was sharp, but tears welled up in her eyes. She reached out and grabbed me by the collar. She tried to talk, but stopped and let go of my shirt. "Liam, just go back to your old life. Go back to the beach." She closed her eyes for a brief moment. "It's going to be all right." I didn't know if she was talking to me or to herself. "Really. It will be." She wiped her eyes, then walked down the hall to her room.

Both Marie and Isabelle, in different ways, had asked me to leave well enough alone. I didn't want to be in the dark. I walked to the desk where Marie had been working. On a notepad I saw she had written a single word: "Kiyan." I picked up the pad and noticed that my hand shook. Something was going on between the Kiyans and Marie. I thought back to the look she gave them at his funeral. I sat down in my dad's leather chair and tried to put everything together, but nothing added up. I had a lot of questions, and I knew I wouldn't like any of the answers. I could have gone to Marie's room and asked her what the Kiyans had to do with her and Archibald Roth, but I knew that I wouldn't get a straight answer. So, I decided to drive out to their farm myself.

As I climbed into my truck, I saw Dane Lohan driving up to the house in his unmarked police cruiser, which might as well have been painted black and white with the siren blasting. Everyone in La Bolsa knew what the detectives drove. Dane pulled up next to me, and we exchanged greetings. He told me Eddie Capuano's parents had claimed the body, but there would be no funeral, no service to honor him. Eddie didn't have a friend in the world other than a few bums who camped out near the pier.

"You really think he killed my dad?"

He nodded. "There's no doubt."

"But the police have been wrong before."

"Not this time." He scratched at his nose. "Just what did Eddie tell you?"

"That he didn't do it. That he wasn't the only one on the pier that night."

He laughed. "Yeah, that's original. He told us the same thing, Liam. You don't think we know how to do our job? We checked up on it. Nada."

"Something's not right, Dane. I don't think Eddie killed himself. I don't think he had the strength to do it. None of it makes sense to me."

"I've never seen a murder that made any sense." He took off his sunglasses and glared at me. "I've seen these things before. He took his own life. Just mind your own business. I know what I'm doing. I've been a cop for a while now." Dane rubbed his hand against his forehead. "I'm sorry. I'm pissed those guards didn't watch him better. I shouldn't take it out on you."

He drummed his fingers on the steering wheel for a second. "Hey, is Marie home?"

"She's inside. I'll see you around."

"Where're you off to?"

I almost told him, but thought better of it. I didn't need Dane to know that I still had questions about my father's murder. "Down to the beach. The surf looks good."

"Sure does. You forgot your board, though." He grinned at me. "There's nothing new to find. Just let it go, Liam. I know it's hard, but you have to let it go."

He knew I wasn't done with this. "I get it," I said. "The case is closed."

"That's right, Liam. It's closed. Don't go looking for something that isn't there."

I gave him a wave and headed down the driveway. In my rearview mirror I saw Dane watching me until I drove out of his line of sight.

CHAPTER FOURTEEN

TRASH AND BRANCHES spread out on the road, creating an obstacle course that slowed traffic. A fire truck raced in the opposite direction without its siren on. I guessed the fire department was searching out potential hot spots for fires.

Driving down PCH, I could see that the water was packed with surfers. A lot of us blamed Gidget or Frankie and Annette for the increased crowds that blanketed the beach. That was partially true, but surfboards were also getting lighter and cheaper, both to make and to buy. It proved less difficult for Valley boys to take up the sport. It created a lot of tension, and some surfers, like Bobby Dix, took on any outsider who dared surf *their* waves. Territory was being staked out, and lines were being drawn. And while most surfers railed against the painfully stupid beach movies, many had no trouble taking money from the Hollywood people as extras and stunt doubles. Even Miki "Da Cat" Dora wasn't above it. Even pure watermen wanted in on the cash.

I turned off the highway and passed the Sol Vista development site, where my father had been building residential homes on former marshlands. A giant billboard greeted prospective buyers. It showed a family barbequing in their backyard, the blue ocean behind them, a smiling dolphin in the air: "Live the Dream! Houses start at $23,500!"

Though he helped build La Bolsa into what it was today, he still had faced a tough battle to develop the site. My father had told me the biggest hurdle he'd needed to overcome was from Dawn, who'd led a group opposed to building on the marsh. In fact, she'd almost stopped him until two city council members had suddenly changed their votes. I thought he'd hate her for what she had tried to do, but her actions had impressed him. "She got people interested in saving a stinking swamp. Can you believe that?" he'd laughed. "I could use someone like Dawn. She's one smart girl."

The wood frames were up for the model house, and tractors and bulldozers were clearing the way for more than three hundred future homes. My dad had often tried to get me interested in his plans for La Bolsa. I had pretended to like what he wanted to do—make La Bolsa into a real thriving city—but it wasn't anything I could get excited about. La Bolsa was home, and I saw no need to change it into something different.

I drove a few more miles and saw the sign for the Kiyan Farms. I passed their fruit stand, but didn't recognize anyone working it, and then I turned left onto a dirt road, past a few Japanese men picking strawberries, sweat soaking through their shirts. I'd never been here before. The Kiyans lived in a small farmhouse fronted by a swarm of cherry blossom trees. I pulled up into their driveway and saw Bonnie's little sister, Joy, reading a book on a bench next to a small man-made pond. She must have been a high school junior by now. She didn't go to La Bolsa High School; they had her enrolled in a private school, as they were very protective of her. I waved to her, but as soon as Joy saw me, she walked quickly into the house.

I stayed in the truck for a moment, debating exactly what I wanted to know from Mrs. Kiyan. Why had she stayed in the background at my father's funeral? What did her family have to do with my sister and Archibald Roth? I knew a little about them. Mr. Kiyan's father had purchased the land shortly after arriving in California just after the turn of the century, and he'd turned it into a farm growing mostly strawberries. The Kiyans seemed to live in their own world, one that kept them apart from everyone else. I'd heard Bonnie was working on her doctorate at UCLA, leaving only Joy, her mother, and a few cousins living and working on the farm.

During World War II, the Kiyans had been interned at Manzanar, one of the Japanese relocation camps, forcing them to give up the farm. After their release, somehow they were able to reclaim their farm and get it back up and running in no time. Mr. Kiyan died about sixteen years ago after a long battle with cancer, and Joy wasn't born until shortly thereafter. I didn't know which would be worse: never knowing your father, or knowing him and having him die, leaving you with a hole in your heart that would never be filled.

Sitting in my truck and roasting in the heat wasn't getting me anywhere, nor had anyone come out of the house to greet me. I started to think that my visit was a stupid idea. Seeing Joy Kiyan flee from the sight of me, like I was some kind of boogeyman, didn't make me feel welcome, either. My palms felt damp and my stomach seemed to house a hive-full of bumblebees. I knew I was intruding on their lives, but I knew, too, that somehow our lives were tied together. Their home seemed to be from another land and time. As I approached their front door, I noticed a small Buddha incense holder on the porch. The scent of jasmine enveloped the air around me.

I knocked gently on the door. I heard movement and voices inside. Mrs. Kiyan spoke to Joy in Japanese, her voice stern and firm. I knew Mrs. Kiyan was born and raised in Japan, and I'd heard rumors that her marriage to Mr. Kiyan had been arranged by both of their parents. I couldn't fathom marrying a relative stranger and then leaving the only place you ever knew, probably never to see your family again.

She opened the door. Mrs. Kiyan looked like a Japanese version of Donna Reed. I don't think I had ever noticed how attractive she was. She had on a pink skirt with a short-sleeved white blouse and a pearl necklace. Andy Williams' "Almost There" played on the radio. She gave me a tight smile, but didn't say a word.

"Hi, Mrs. Kiyan. It's Liam Sol. I wondered if we could talk for a moment."

"About what?" Her voice was soft and with barely a trace of an accent.

"My father."

Her expression didn't change, but I felt as if I had crossed some kind of line.

"I don't understand."

"I saw you, and Bonnie, and Joy at his funeral—"

She cut me off. "I'm sorry, but I cannot help you."

"Actually, I think you might be able to."

"You must go now. Please."

She started to shut the door, but without thinking, I put my hand up and stopped it from closing on me.

"Mrs. Kiyan. Can I talk to Bonnie?"

I could tell my action had frightened her, so I dropped my hand.

"She is not here."

"Can you tell me where I can find her?"

"You have to leave now, or I will have no choice but to call the police." Her voice shook. I stepped back from the door. "Thank you," she said. Mrs. Kiyan gave me a small bow and shut the door and locked it.

I felt like crap. The only thing I had accomplished was to scare Joy and her mother. I turned and walked back to the truck where two of her cousins waited for me. Neither appeared very happy about my presence.

I didn't know these guys. They were complete opposites in appearance but both with well-toned muscles from working in the fields. One was short and round with a thick mustache and long hair. The other was clean-shaven, about my height, with a crew cut. They seemed eager to take me on. I'd never really been in a fight before, just little scuffles that were quickly broken up before they got out of hand.

"What do you want?" the shorter one asked. He had a thick accent. I tried to think of a way to get by them and to my truck. The taller guy followed me and was now just a few feet behind me. The other stationed himself directly between me and the truck. His legs parted slightly as if he were ready to attack.

"Nothing. I was just leaving."

The short one scowled at me. "Nothing? You scare Joy and upset Mrs. Kiyan. Can't be nothing."

I sensed the tall one closing in on me. I put my hands up to indicate that I was sorry.

"I didn't mean to scare anyone. I—"

Suddenly the tall one grabbed me and pinned my arms behind me. The short one came up to me. His breath smelled like dead fish.

"You don't come around here. Got that? You leave Joy and Mrs. Kiyan alone."

"I'm sorry, okay? I like them. I don't want to upset anyone."

"Good. Then you don't come back anymore." He nodded at the tall guy. He released me, then, before I could move, he grabbed me again and tripped me to the ground. I tried to get up, but the shorter one kicked me hard in the ribs; the pain felt like an electric jolt setting fire to every nerve in my body. A second kick connected with my stomach, the air sucked out of my lungs as if through a vacuum.

I crawled toward the truck, my fingers digging into the gravel as I tried desperately to catch my breath. The shorter one followed me, patted me on the head, and then threw another kick to my ribs. I heard myself whimper, just like a goddamned baby. He kept kicking me like I was a stray dog. I put my hand up to wave him off, and I realized I would have done most anything to make him stop. When I made it to my truck, he pulled me up by my shirt collar, and he grabbed my face with his hand and shook it. "You come around here again, I kill you. No lying. I kill you." He shoved me against the car door. "Go," he said. "Go."

I got in and pulled the keys out of my pocket. My hands shook so much that I had a difficult time putting the key in the ignition. I glanced behind me, making sure they weren't coming after me again. A curtain pulled back from one of the windows of the house, revealing Mrs. Kiyan, her hand covering her mouth.

I drove down Santa Anita Canyon Road toward the beach. After a few miles I pulled over to the side. I rested my head on the steering wheel and tried to breathe. The pain was searing. My ribs burned, and I felt like I was going to throw up. I stumbled out of my truck, but I held on to the door as if it were a life preserver. I tried to catch my breath as my heart pounded. I slid to the ground and tucked my knees up to my chest, wincing again from the pain. I felt humiliated and ashamed of myself for being so easy to bully.

I knew I couldn't have held my own against them, but why hadn't I put up some kind of fight? Thrown a punch? Anything but cower like a scared child? I couldn't chase the whimpering sound I had made out of my head. What would my father have thought of me now? I tried not to think what his answer might have been.

I sat on the curb for a while, the gutter water beneath me rushing its way to a nearby storm drain. Cars breezed by, fragments of songs from their radios trailing behind them in the wind. After a while, I got up and dusted myself off. I wanted to cry. I'd scared the hell out of Mrs.

Kiyan, gotten my ass kicked by strawberry pickers, had my manhood stripped from me, and it wasn't even noon yet. Maybe Marie and Dane were right. Maybe I needed to go back to the beach.

CHAPTER FIFTEEN

I COULD NOT BRING myself to go back to my parents' house. This morning's humiliation churned in my gut. I wanted to be alone. My family thought I was a flake anyway, so I figured it didn't matter if I showed up or not.

Dexter's Bar sat between a shoe repair place and a beauty parlor just off Main Street in La Bolsa. No tourists ever stopped here. This wasn't a place a person would stumble upon. It was a destination, strictly a place for locals. Either you were hiding out from something or someone, or you were a biker or a surfer who just came for a little peace. While neither population mixed very well, trouble never found its way to Dexter's. It served as a demilitarized zone. In fact, we referred to it as the DMZ.

No one wanted to mess with Dexter. A decorated veteran of World War II and Korea, Dex made John Wayne look like Cary Grant. His was a place you could go for a drink without the worry of getting hassled, which was exactly what I needed.

The DMZ wasn't, as Dawn and I used to joke, "a clean and well-lighted place." I think Dex liked that his establishment was dark and damp and carried the lingering scent of mold. It kept out the undesirables.

Pictures of surfers hung on the wall: Corky Carroll, Da Bull, Mike

Doyle, and others who had stopped in for a drink. He even had one of me in a very unflattering moment. I remembered the day. We were riding the effects of a hurricane off Baja and the waves were insane. My timing was crap that morning due to a killer hangover. The photograph captured me in the air, flying off of my board, my trunks down to my knees, the wave exploding below, and me looking as if attempting to kiss my own ass good-bye. Despite my objections, Dex kept the picture up. It made him smile and not too much ever made him do that.

I finished off my third tequila with a beer chaser, and while the drinks had calmed me down a bit, I still felt like a wuss. Only one other person sat at the bar, his face resting comfortably in a bowl of peanuts. Two others huddled together in a corner booth, their faces hidden in the shadows, their voices low. You saw a lot of that at the DMZ. Men who cheated on their wives brought their girlfriends here; other men liked to drink in the dark so their friends wouldn't see that they spent their days looking at the bottom of a shot glass. Dex brought me another Coors and poured another shot of tequila. I thanked him and he just laughed. He could never separate me from the photograph. At least I made someone happy.

The scent of cinnamon greeted me, and I glanced to my side. Raven Andrews, looking both lost and found, took the stool next to me.

"Wow, Liam. You look like shit." She gave me the once-over. "You wear it well, though."

"Seems to suit me these days, doesn't it?"

Raven kissed my cheek. "Shut up, Liam."

Dex came up to take her order.

"Well, well, well, what do I feel like? Beer, wine, martini—"

Dex sighed and slapped a bottle of Coors in front of her. The customer didn't come first at the DMZ.

"Beer it is," she said, giving him a wink.

Dex then poured her a shot of tequila.

Raven picked up the shot glass and finished the tequila off in one gulp, then took a long sip of her beer, her eyes focused on mine the whole time.

"How are you doing, Liam?"

I stared at my drinks and tried to come up with a response, but I had nothing. Her hand found my knee, her touch gentle and comforting.

"I don't know," I said.

She looked at me, her eyes encouraging me to continue.

"I want it to be last month. That's what it is. I want it to be last month."

Her hand went from my knee to my hand, and she held it tight.

"I miss my dad." I paused for a second. "There's shit going on with my family. Something they don't want me to know. And whatever it is, I don't want to know it, I don't. But I can't stop myself. I need to find out what it is."

I started to take a sip of the tequila, but stopped. "I... backed down from a fight today. I just crawled away on my hands and knees, like a coward. I didn't even stand up on my own two feet."

"Who was it?"

"I don't know their names."

" 'Their?' There was more than one?"

I nodded my head.

"Men are so goddamned stupid. You feel bad because you didn't take on two guys? I call that being smart."

"It's more than that."

I looked around to make sure no one else could hear me. The two guys in the back corner were immersed in their own conversation. I wondered what private sins they had confessed to each other.

"I'm scared and I don't know what I'm scared of."

"Losing your dad, it must change how you see things."

"Eddie Capuano didn't kill my father."

"How do you know that?"

"He told me he didn't. I know it's stupid, but I… I believe him. I don't think Eddie had it in him to kill anyone."

"Who did it then?"

I shook my head.

"Someone had a reason."

I didn't know why I confided in her. I downed the tequila and then finished off the rest of my beer. Raven moved the barstool closer to me, our thighs touching, her head resting on my shoulder.

"Life is never what we want it to be, Liam. We have to take what it gives us, I guess. Sometimes we don't have a choice."

She turned to me. Her blue eyes moist, as if she saw something from her own life that she wanted to leave behind, but couldn't.

She leaned over and kissed me, her mouth warm and inviting.

"Take me home, Liam."

Before I could respond, she said, "Your home."

As I opened the door for Raven, a splash of sunlight fell on the two men seated in the corner booth. Archibald Roth nodded his head in recognition, grinning smugly, as if he knew something about me that I didn't. Next to him sat Dawn's boyfriend. He lowered his head, avoiding eye contact, either out of shame or because he didn't want to be recognized.

"What is it, Liam?" Raven asked.

"Let's go home," I said. The last thing I needed was to do any more thinking. "My home."

CHAPTER SIXTEEN

THE PALE-FACED MAN

THEY WERE LAUGHING as they entered the house. They were joined at the lips, their hands roaming all over each other. Then she pushed him up against the wall and kissed him hard on the mouth.

"Careful," the surfer said, "my ribs hurt like hell."

"Oh, I'm sorry, Liam," the girl said. Then she gently kissed his chest.

She pulled off her top and tossed it to the floor. Like a typical hippie chick, she wasn't wearing a bra. She unbuttoned his shirt and softly pressed her body up against his and then slid her tongue into his ear.

"Let's go to the bedroom," the surfer boy said.

"No," the girl said. "Let's do it here."

Their voices sounded like a mix of desperation and lust. The surfer smiled and grabbed her hand and led her back to his bedroom. The pale-faced man heard them fall onto the bed, followed by more giggles.

They never knew he was there. He had that gift. The pale-faced man was sitting on the floor behind the leather chair, invisible but still in plain view.

He'd been in the house well before they arrived, waiting. He was told the surfer boy was still asking questions. Still wouldn't let it go. They wanted him to scare the surfer off. He thought killing the surfer would be easier, but he'd been ordered just to give him a good scare. He could do that. He was good at that.

The place smelled like the beach. The pale-faced man inspected the house, knowing they wouldn't hear him. A small side patio, where the guy kept his surfboards, sat just outside the kitchen. The sound of the oil wells pumping outside the windows wasn't so bad. He liked the off-kilter rhythm it produced. The crashing of waves bothered him, though. He knew that some found the pounding of the waves peaceful, but he found it disturbing.

He walked back out to the living rom. The surfer liked to read. There were books stacked in the makeshift bookcase and also on the floor: Kerouac, Ian Fleming, Hemingway, Twain, some Eastern philosophy bullshit, mysteries, and science fiction. He picked up one of the books, *Free Fall* by William Golding, and thumbed through it. On the inside cover was a handwritten note: *Passages of this book remind me of the late night talks we had while lying on the beach. I love you, Liam, more than you can possibly know. Dawn.* He noticed a framed picture of the surfer with a pretty brunette. He guessed the picture had been taken when they were teenagers. He wondered if the girl in the picture was Dawn. It wasn't the hippie chick the surfer was balling in the bedroom. He held the picture and starred at the girl's face. He saw a depth to her that unsettled him. He put the picture back before giving it one last look. The pale-faced man didn't know why, but the picture made him hate the surfer.

He walked down the hallway and stood outside the bedroom door and watched them fuck. He could tell it wasn't their first time together. They knew how to get each other going. The pale-faced man observed them a while longer and then grew restless.

He walked into the living room, but couldn't sit still. He wanted to charge into the bedroom and scare them right now, when the surfer would be most vulnerable, but he knew he couldn't be seen. He needed to be a shadow.

He went outside and sat on one of the chairs on the front porch. He lit a cigarette and took in the dark night and then felt himself begin to calm down.

He didn't like either of them. The girl was a hippie and he hated hippies. Peace, love, and freeloading. But the surfer got to him on a different level. The guy didn't work, as far as he could tell. And he knew that pretty girls just fell into the surfer's lap. The surfer had that confidence, the thing that boys of privilege always had, whether they consciously knew it or not—they knew the world was theirs and everyone else were just their guests. He took a deep drag off his cigarette and then exhaled slowly and watched the smoke disappear into the night.

He checked his watch. They'd be here in a few hours. He didn't know how he would use them yet, but he knew they'd put a good scare into the hippie chick and the surfer. But if the two separated, he was going to let his new friends take care of the girl. He wanted the surfer to himself.

CHAPTER SEVENTEEN

SEX WAS NEVER a game with Raven. It just worked. Our bodies found each other, and sometimes we'd stumble and make wrong moves, but we'd laugh and then once again find our rhythm and our sense. It wasn't about the future or the past, only about the present. The bed springs squeaked in time with the oil wells until I collapsed on top of her. She wrapped herself tighter around me and held on just a bit longer until she let out a soft moan. After a moment, her arms fell to her side, and we both forgot the things that were hurting us, at least for a little while. And afterward, unlike how it felt with most girls, I didn't want Raven to leave.

"You know why you like being with me?"

I traced my fingers slowly around her breasts. "Because it's fun."

"Because you don't love me. You like me and you trust me. But you'll never love me. And that's the way you like it."

"I don't know about that."

She grabbed my hand. "It's okay, Liam. I'm not looking for a ring. It's fun to be with you. We're a good time together, but you don't want to be with a girl who you might fall in love with. That's all I'm saying."

Raven held my face in her hands and gave me a long slow kiss.

"Hold me," she said.

I drew her close to me until I could feel her heartbeat, soft and steady and flowing evenly with the lilt of her breathing, and soon she drifted off into a deep sleep. I kept her in my arms, closed my eyes, and tried not to think about what she had just told me.

I didn't see Raven when I woke up. Darkness filled the room. It was just after five in the morning. A faint trace of cinnamon settled in the air, as if she had inhabited my room for a brief moment a long time ago. It wasn't like Raven to hang around. Still, I was disappointed to see that she might have left. I got out of bed hoping that she was still here.

I glanced inside the living room, but there was no sign of Raven. I went into the kitchen to make some coffee. The Santa Ana winds kept the house hot, so I opted for a cold bottle of Double Cola instead. I leaned against the counter and put the bottle next to my cheek, the chill feeling good against my face. I thought about what Raven had said about why we weren't more than what we were. We made each other laugh, and we shared a strong attraction, no doubt. But I had never for a moment pictured us as a couple. It had never entered my mind. I heard the sound of the front door open and the screen door shutting behind it.

"You're back," I said, as I walked out to the living room. The front door was open, but no one was there. I scanned the hall toward my bedroom, though I knew she wasn't there. Was someone else in the house?

I approached the screen door, and caught the smell of cigarette smoke. It was strong and now instantly recognizable: cloves. I felt the hairs on the back of my neck start to rise.

"Raven?"

I peered out the screen door, but darkness owned the early morning. I tried to turn on the porch light, but the bulb must have burned out. "Raven?"

Something moved behind one of the bushes that dotted my front yard.

"Who's there?"

"Who's there?" The reply came back in a falsetto voice, mocking me. "You sure gave it to her tonight, huh?" The tone of his voice turned husky. It sounded like phlegm had mined itself deep into his lungs. "Made me jealous."

I couldn't make him out. He was just a shadow in my front yard, but there was something familiar about him. I thought for a second that it might be one of the guys who tossed me around at the Kiyan farms, but this guy didn't have an accent.

He lit a cigarette, which allowed me a quick glimpse of his face. He resembled the pale-faced guy at Rosa's.

"Who are you?"

"No one you want to know."

"What do you want? Where's Raven?"

I slid my hand down and locked the screen door. I knew it wouldn't hold anyone back, yet it made me feel safer.

"Shame about Eddie Capuano, wasn't it?"

"What do you mean?"

"Nothing. Just probably didn't have to happen, that's all."

A lone drop of sweat slid down the middle of my back.

"You killed Eddie?"

"Maybe you killed him," he said.

"You'd better leave now or I'll call the—"

"The police? You don't know much, do you? You know, you got a good life, surfer boy. Rich family, pretty girlfriends who don't have their legs tied shut, your health—be a shame to lose all that."

"What do you want?"

He tossed the cigarette onto the porch. The black stub lay there like a lit fuse.

"Where's Raven?" I asked.

"She's in good hands."

"If anything happens to her—"

"You'll do what? Understand this: Eddie Capuano killed your dad. And now he's dead. Just back off. There's nothing to see here, so just go back to the beach, surfer boy. We don't want anyone else to end up like your friend Eddie."

"Where is she?"

No response.

"Where is she?"

I heard him laugh in the distance, and then a motorcycle started up and rode off. I waited until I could no longer hear the engine, then ran to the kitchen and called Dane Lohan at home. He answered on the first ring, but he must have placed his palm over the phone. I thought I heard a second voice in the background whispering to him. Finally, he barked out a "hello." I told him what had happened.

He said he'd be right over. I couldn't help but notice a slight tremble in his voice.

While I waited for Dane to arrive, I inspected the house. I was scared and worried about Raven. I wanted to clean everything. Just knowing that guy had broken inside my house, and what he'd seen and heard, made me feel sick and, oddly, ashamed. Had he waited here for me or had he followed us?

Out on the front porch, I started to change the light bulb, but found that it had been unscrewed. This guy thought of everything. I tightened the bulb and the light came on. I was sure the guy had left, but I felt vulnerable, like easy prey. I went out to the front yard, where he had been hiding. Everything appeared to be normal, then I noticed three black cigarette butts lying on the ground, each one smoked exactly halfway down. I felt cold now, and I took a seat on the front porch and waited for Dane and, hopefully, Raven.

He arrived at my house minutes later. Dane tucked in his shirt as he emerged from the car, breathing hard like he had just completed a marathon. He was on edge, jittery as if a dose of amphetamines had been injected into his veins.

"You said on the phone that you may have seen this guy before?"

"Yes, and it sounded like he needed to cough up his lungs."

"Yeah?" Dane grimaced. "What'd he say he wanted?"

"He didn't say. He just said it was too bad about Eddie Capuano, that he didn't have to die. And he threatened me."

He nodded his head. "And you think he kidnapped Raven?"

"I don't know, but where the hell did she go?"

"Did you hear a scream or anything?"

I told him I hadn't.

"Raven's probably fine. I don't think he would have harmed or kidnapped her and then hung around just to chat with you."

"We weren't chatting, Dane."

"I know. I know."

"Dane, why would he mention Eddie Capuano?"

He didn't answer.

"He didn't even care if I called the police. Do you know who this guy is?" He didn't respond. "Dane?"

"I wouldn't read too much into it. The fact that Eddie Capuano murdered your father and then killed himself is pretty well known."

"I think this guy may have killed Eddie, Dane."

"He was probably just taunting you. Where did you find the cigarettes?"

I showed him the one on the porch, and then we walked out to the front yard. Dane stopped me. "The other thing, Liam, is that Raven's been known to hang around some pretty undesirable types. One of these guys could have followed the two of you home."

"Yes, Raven can attract a strange brew, but this guy was different. This guy was here about me."

"I don't know what to tell you," Dane said. He bent down and examined the cigarettes. He moved the butts around with a twig he had picked up from the ground. "Are you sure these are his?"

"He stood right there, smoking. I think I saw this guy at Rosa's before."

"Rosa's, huh?" He kept looking at the cigarettes. "Black clove. Some of the hippies like smoking these. It can help mask the smell of marijuana."

"I wouldn't call a cop out here if I'd been toking on a joint, Dane."

"Do you want to file a report?"

"I want the cops to look for her. Raven may be in danger."

"Why would I be in any danger?"

Raven had that kind of timing. She gave me a smile, but I could tell she wasn't happy to see Dane. I was relieved as hell to see her, though.

Her arms hugged her chest as she walked up to the front porch.

Dane patted me on the shoulder. "Liam tells me you two had a visitor tonight. He thought something might have happened to you."

She gave a shrug. "I just walked down to Johnny-Bob's to get some donuts for us, but they weren't open yet."

Johnny-Bob's was a donut place on PCH. They were supposed to open up at five every morning, but Johnny-Bob was notoriously unreliable. Sometimes he didn't open until noon.

"Anyone bother you?" Dane asked.

She turned to me. "What's going on?"

He looked at her hard and then at me. "Did you want to file the complaint?"

"I'll think about it," I said.

"Listen, I doubt if he'll come by again, but I'll make sure to have a patrol car cruise by on the hour." Dane scanned the grounds and then walked to his car. I couldn't help but notice that he appeared more relieved about Raven showing up safely than I did.

"God, I'm glad to see you." She ran to me and I gave her a hug. And then she fell limp in my arms.

"Raven, why did you leave?"

"Liam." Her voice sounded flat and void of emotion.

"Someone was here. I think he watched us. He may have been in the house, too. It's sick. He threatened me out here and—"

"Liam."

I could feel her head pushing against my shoulder. "What?"

"They threatened me, Liam."

"Who?"

"I was going to Johnny-Bob's, and these guys on motorcycles stopped me. I've never seen them before. They asked me if I ever wanted to have children. They touched me. They told me to keep my mouth shut. They told me you'd better just back off, or..." Raven's voice trailed off and she started to shake. I held her tighter and felt her shudder in my arms.

"I have to let Dane know now."

"You can't. They said they'd come back for me."

"Do you know who these guys are? Have you seen them before?"

She shook her head. "Some biker gang, I guess. They weren't from around here." Raven began to cry.

I felt that every action I took only resulted in messing up someone's life.

The sun peeked over the water and with it came the hot winds, which had infiltrated the house. Still, I lit a fire in the fireplace, and Raven wrapped herself in a blanket on the couch. I made some coffee and put The Lovin' Spoonful's *Daydream* album on the stereo. Dawn had bought the record as a birthday present for me. She'd said listening to it always made her feel better. Listening to it now only reminded me of Dawn, and at one time in my life that had been a good thing.

I hoped it would make Raven feel better. Yet the happiness of *Daydream* seemed to mock me now. The songs held a promise I had once bought into, but now it was a joke. I thought about changing records, but Raven seemed comforted by the music.

I sat across from her in an old leather chair that had come with the place. When I first moved in, it sat alone next to the fireplace. Barnabas McCaig, the man who lived here before me, worked in the oil fields. One day, for no apparent reason, he left and took everything with him, leaving only the leather chair behind. No one knew where he had gone off to or why. His rent had been paid up for the whole year. Lately, I had been thinking of disappearing. Nothing serious, but the thoughts, though brief, appeared more often now. I thought about Barnabas. Wherever he was, I hoped he had freed himself from whatever had driven him away. Still, I wondered if he just plain disliked the chair or meant to leave it as a gift to the next occupant. I had purchased some decent furniture over the years, but whenever I felt troubled, the old chair always proved to be a source of comfort.

Raven was fast asleep. She said she didn't know who had attacked her, but like the guy in the yard, they knew who we were. Her assault had everything to do with me. And while those guys assaulted Raven, another one threatened me in my front yard. The Kiyans didn't have to send anyone out to warn me. They'd made their point. I had no plans to bother them again. The only other people I had talked to were Dane, my mother, and my sisters. Why would anyone care if I had questions about my father's death?

I knew I should call the police again, but Raven's reaction frightened me. Maybe I could talk to Dane, just to let him know what had happened, but maybe that would jeopardize Raven's safety. I couldn't let anything else happen to her.

The early morning light peered in through the windows. I rose from the chair and walked outside to the front yard to clear my head. Somebody had killed my father, and may have killed Eddie Capuano. I wanted to find who had taken my father's life, but the thought of taking another step forward scared the hell out of me. I knew that if anyone in my family had been killed, my father would not have rested until he found the murderer. I wasn't my father; I knew that. Having any harm come to Raven was something I couldn't live with. It had to stop now. It was time to let go. I should have felt relieved, but instead I felt like a coward.

CHAPTER EIGHTEEN

THE WINDS HAD passed a few weeks ago, and we were settling into the cold of November. Lonnie, Hike, and I were in Puerto Nuevo, about an hour south of the border. Our annual trip down to Baja couldn't have come at a better time. It had taken me a while to get back in the water and on the waves, and we were riding a beautiful swell. At first I'd found myself dropping out of the head-high waves—my timing wrong, or the face now, suddenly, appeared too steep for me. What once got me stoked now played games with my head. Gun-shy, I couldn't let myself go. I decided to start off on the smaller, inside waves, the type of waves that I hadn't ridden since I was a little grommet. Slowly, I let the rhythm of the water find me and cleanse me, and then, hopefully, like a baptism, save me. Soon I was paddling out to the bigger waves, and then it all came back. Just me and the water—we tested each other, we played, and then, when we were at our best, we became one.

I liked being in Baja this time of year as there were fewer surfers here compared to Southern California. I thought about writing something for *Surf's Up!* It had been much too long since I had penned any stories for them, and I found I had missed that as well.

Life was getting back to normal, though I knew it would never be like before. I still thought I had betrayed my father, but since I had stopped asking questions, no one had bothered me or Raven.

Instead of drawing Raven and me closer, the events of that night drew us apart. No more nights were spent together, and when we did see each other, we acted overly polite. She no longer wore the cinnamon scent I identified with her. I could only assume that it ushered back memories of the one night she had felt completely helpless. Now, the aroma she once loved bore the lingering memory of violence. I never felt good seeing Raven after that. She only reminded me that I couldn't protect her—that being with me for that one night could have killed her, and that now she would never again feel as safe as she once did.

We were grilling fresh lobster that we'd bought from a local fisherman over our campfire, along with some fish that Lonnie had caught. Lonnie's fishing abilities were like none that I'd ever seen. *Field and Stream* could learn a lot from him.

"You have to let them know that your presence is pure," he said. "We are all of the water. Except they taste better than we do."

"That's why we let you come along," Hike told him. "The Pied Piper of fish, you are."

"Hey, man," Lonnie said. "The only reason we bring you along, Hike, is in case we ever need to trade you for our freedom."

"He'd be a horrible hostage," I added. "No one would pay a dime of ransom for him."

"And we'd be out of Dodge before they realized they'd been had."

The sun touched the horizon as a pod of dolphin rode the waves in our absence. Sometimes they'd ride with us, but this group liked to surf solo. They were beautiful to watch—graceful, pure, and at home in the sea.

"They're the true watermen," I said. "You ever see these guys at Marineland? It makes me sick."

"I know," Lonnie said. "It's sad. Trap them up in a big fish tank and make them do tricks."

"Have either of you read *Planet of the Apes*?" I asked.

Hike smiled. "I don't read, college boy. Hmmm... maybe that will be my excuse."

"For what?"

"I got a notice in the mail."

"Shit," I said. The one letter we all dreaded receiving. I'd never told them about the notice I got and how my dad had said that he'd take care of it. I still hadn't heard anything since, and I'd never asked my dad any further about it.

"That's right. Uncle Sam wants me to join his team. But I bet he doesn't want an illiterate." He shook his head. "They call it the Selective Service. It can't be very selective if they want me."

Hike pulled a bottle of Tecate from the ice chest. "I know some people who went to Canada. There's no surf, I guess, but I won't be sent to die in some country I've never heard of before, either." He took a long sip of his beer. "Fucking Canada, though. I hate hockey. And don't even get me started on curling."

"I don't get this war," I said. "What did they do to us?"

"It's the domino principle," Hike said. "We have to stop the Commies there, before they get us here."

Lonnie gazed into the flames. "My grandmother plays dominos. No young people play it, just old people. It's *all* a game to them." He checked the fish on the grill. "I'm thinking about enlisting. It feels like I should."

"You want my letter? You can tell them that you're me. Not as good looking, of course, but you can tell them that you've been real sick lately."

"We're all going to get the letter, Hike. What about you, Liam?"

"I don't know. Not much you can do when you get the letter."

"You can always run," Hike said.

Yes, I thought, *I'm good at that.*

Hike shrugged. "Maybe they won't take me. I don't think I could kill anyone, could you? I mean, could you actually pull the trigger?"

"I don't know," I said. "I guess at some point it's either them or you."

It was dark now, after midnight. The dolphins were staying up late, and I could hear them playing in the waves. Hike and Lonnie had fallen asleep, their faces barely illuminated by the dying flames of our fire. I thought about a former surfing buddy of mine, Jason Flay. He went to Nam. He still served there, but when he came home on leave a few months ago, he wasn't the same—something was missing. You couldn't see it with your eyes or hear it. But you could feel it, and it made you a little frightened. It made you realize there were things out there that were beyond comprehension, and that once you had witnessed them, you'd change. You wouldn't be sure how it had changed you—it would be like losing something you never knew you possessed, leaving you feeling unsettled and paranoid. And even in the safety of your own home, you'd always want to look back over your shoulder, just in case.

I thought about Lonnie and Hike going off to Vietnam while I stayed safely behind. "Guess the government didn't have my address," I would say. Just how much bullshit could I live with? Just how many things could I close my eyes to? I didn't even want to know.

The dolphins were gone now, and except for the waves, the only sound I heard was a seagull flying overhead. I crawled into my sleeping bag and stared up at the moonless sky until I could no longer keep my eyes open.

CHAPTER NINETEEN

I SAT WITH MY mother and sisters in the courtyard of my parents' home, drinking coffee and taking in the late Sunday afternoon sun. I'd just returned from Mexico, and I felt as if I'd left the memories of death and assault behind me. Today was Isabelle's birthday. It was a quiet celebration, the only kind she would allow. Ever since she was a teenager, Isabelle never liked anyone to make a fuss when it came to her birthday. She'd rather we all forget about it. Still, Marie had wanted to make it a big deal—and invite donors and supporters of Glenn's run for state Senate—but Isabelle had put her foot down. Glenn ended up leaving the party early anyway to attend a campaign event. My visits to the house were getting easier. I felt as if I had been rewarded for returning to my old self. Even Marie acted happy to see me.

"How was Mexico?" she asked.

"Bitchin'. Just what the doctor ordered."

"I've always wanted to surf," Isabelle said. "You should teach me sometime."

"I don't know if that's the image we want to present to voters, Isabelle. One surfer in the family is enough."

"Goodness, Marie. You're starting to sound like your father. If

Isabelle wants to surf, let her," my mother said. "God knows that life is always shorter and a bit quicker than we'd all like it to be."

"She can surf all she wants after the election."

"Enough of this." My mom waved her hands in the air. "I'll be inside if you need me."

Her pace had slowed, and I noticed she appeared to be more hunched over than I'd ever seen, as if she were literally carrying the weight of the world on her shoulders.

"What do you do in that country, anyway?" Marie asked me.

"Drugs, highway robbery, knock-off banks. All those things that will help Glenn get elected."

Isabelle laughed and Marie smiled.

"I deserved that. Did Raven go to Mexico with you?"

I brushed off her question with a nonchalant "no." I wondered how Marie even knew that Raven and I had been together. It felt as if every part of my life was an open book and I had no idea who was reading it.

"Good. I never liked her. You could do much better." I waited for her to bring up Dawn's name, but this time she held back.

Later, as the sun was setting and everyone was inside, I took a walk around the grounds. I drifted among the orange trees and sat on an old wooden bench my dad had made. It provided a good view of the ocean, and when I was younger, this was my reading bench. Rick Brant and the Hardy Boys had kept me company here for many afternoons. The fog had begun to roll in, and La Bolsa looked to me like some faraway place that dreaded the impending darkness. I examined the bench, trying to find Erin Parker's name, which I had carved in the fifth grade. She was the love of my life then, though she never knew it. I wasn't able to find her name, but what I did see made my heart stop: three black cigarettes, all smoked exactly halfway down.

The cigarettes weren't fresh, but they didn't appear to be too old, either.

I looked up from the bench and toward the house. This location had a clear view to Marie's bedroom. My first thought was that either this guy had threatened Marie or was stalking her. But why? Marie was the one who didn't want me to pursue my father's death. Of course, he may have just been watching the house, not Marie. Maybe he met someone here. But who? My father? I didn't want to go down this path again. No good was going to come from this. My stomach twisted into a massive knot. I walked around the bench to see if there were any more cigarettes, but I found nothing. But he had been here. He had come to my parents' house. Someone in my family, other than me, might also be in danger.

Back in the house, I looked for my mother. I had to be quiet about things, but I wanted to hang around just to see what I could learn. I found her in the family room, a glass of wine in her hand, watching *Ralph Story's Los Angeles*. Ralph Story always had a unique view of L.A. and of those who lived there. He was introducing a segment about Little Tokyo and spoke of the history of the Japanese in Los Angeles.

"Hey, if it's okay with you, I think I'll spend the night," I said.

She glanced up from the screen. Her eyes were glassy and her jaws were clenched.

"Is everything okay, Liam?"

"Yes, I'm just tired. Plus, it's been a nice day, and I don't want to go home. I want to stay here."

That seemed to cheer her up.

"We'd love to have you." She finished the last of her wine. "I'll have your bed made up for you." She stood up and tried to place her glass on the coffee table. But she missed and it fell, shattering on the hardwood floor.

She bent over to pick up the pieces.

"Let me get those." I knelt down and helped her collect the shards of glass.

"Guess I've had too much to drink today."

She glared at the TV screen. It showed an old picture of Little Tokyo with a young Japanese woman in front of a cherry blossom tree. The woman stood perfectly erect, her face serious, as if she'd never been in a photograph before and wasn't sure what to expect.

"Will you turn the damn thing off, Liam? I think I'll run up to bed. Can you pick up the rest of the glass?"

I told her I would. She cupped the broken glass in her hand and walked toward the kitchen. A small trickle of blood seeped through her fingers.

"Mom, you're bleeding."

She stopped and examined her hand. "Oh, so I am." She smiled at me. "Didn't feel a thing." With that, she left as if nothing had happened. A few drops of her blood fell from her hand to the floor.

After my mom had gone to bed, Isabelle and I played a game of Scrabble out on the courtyard. Marie had gone out to join Glenn at the fundraiser, while Isabelle chose to stay at home.

"You didn't want to go?" I asked her.

"Glenn wanted me there to woo new supporters and voters. I know him. It's about raising money through the art of seduction, but I'd prefer not to be ogled tonight. I don't feel up to it."

The moon hid itself behind the fog, which had settled in for the night. The lanterns that hung over our table gave an orange glow to the letters on the board. The air felt chilly, but we wrapped ourselves in blankets and drank Mexican hot chocolate to help keep us warm.

As I sorted my tiles, I asked Isabelle if she'd noticed if Mom had been drinking more than usual lately.

"It's been rough on her. She acts like everything's back to normal, but it never will be."

"I know," I said.

"I've tried talking to her, but..." Her voice trailed off. "What are you looking at?"

My eyes were focused on the bench where I had found the cigarettes. I didn't expect to see anything, but I couldn't help but think that someone might be out there, watching us."

"Nothing. I'm sorry."

"You sure? You look concerned."

"No. I'm fine."

"She likes it when you're here, you know."

"Mom?"

"I can tell. She's happier when you're around."

"Is everything okay here? No strange guys coming around?"

"Strange men?"

I knew it was a stupid approach, but I never was very good at fishing. "I don't know, with Dad gone I worry about you guys."

"We're fine, more than fine. Besides, we have Marie. Only a fool would mess with her."

Or a psychopath, I thought.

CHAPTER TWENTY

IT FELT STRANGE sleeping in my old room. I remembered when Dawn and I used to sneak up here to fool around. Half drunk, we tried in vain to keep from stumbling on the stairs, stopping every now and then to make out, before finally getting to my room where we awkwardly, but enthusiastically, took off each other's clothes. The things we whispered in each other's ears seemed silly at the time. But I now realized they were truths. Truths that liked to come back every now and then just to taunt me.

Marie and Glenn hadn't come home from the campaign meeting yet. I sat on my bed and gazed out the window. The chances of the guy returning tonight were slim, but I felt compelled to keep my eyes open. I thought about how nice it felt being with my family. They were as relaxed as I had ever seen any of them, though my mother's drinking certainly had me worried.

I rested my head back on the pillow and examined the night sky. An opening appeared in the fog as if someone had taken a knife and sliced through the clouds to reveal the small string of stars that made up the hunter's bow of Orion. A shooting star flew across the opening before disappearing into a layer of the fog. As a kid, falling stars had brought about a sense of magic and wonder, of things not yet seen and waiting to be discovered. Now, they just made me sad, a burnt-out sun's dying gasp. My eyes settled on the stars until the fog slowly covered them in its cold blanket.

He was wrapped in seaweed and struggling in the deep water. I was at P.O.P., riding the Sea Serpent Roller Coaster. He was waving for me. He tried calling out, but I couldn't hear his voice. I was laughing too hard. The dips and drops over the ocean were too much fun. Below me, trucks and bulldozers were tearing down the amusement park, but I kept on riding. I saw the panic in his eyes, but I hoped he could hold out for just a few more minutes—the best part of the ride was coming up, and I didn't want to miss out. I yelled out at him and told him to wait, but I didn't think he heard me over the screams of the young girls holding on for dear life. As we took the last drop, he looked at me, and I could tell that he didn't understand my dilemma. But I knew he'd be all right. Nothing would ever happen to him. But still he couldn't free himself from the seaweed. His face took on the color of a rotting blueberry. It made me want to laugh. I knew I should have gotten off, but the ride was so fun. He'd still be there when it ended. I felt as sure of that as I was sure of anything in this world. Then a hand rose up from below the water, seaweed clinging to its fingers, and it grabbed my father. It pulled him beneath the sea as the coaster screamed off the tracks and I plunged into the wreckage of the park below.

I woke up. My arms clung to the side of the bed. I felt like I was falling from a height I had never before experienced. My stomach settled, and I waited for my heart to stop racing. The dream left me unbalanced. I hadn't meant to fall asleep. I peered out the window, but the night and the fog worked together to make seeing anything nearly impossible. Across the hall, I heard the door to Isabelle's room closing softly.

I went out to the hallway and put an ear to Isabelle's door, and then

I heard voices coming from downstairs. I crept toward the top of the stairway. Two figures stood outside of the front door. They looked like ghosts coming in from the clouds.

"You need to trust me, Glenn."

It was Marie.

"I know what I'm doing."

The figures moved closer together, and whatever light that once stood between them had disappeared.

"I don't want anyone to get hurt," Glenn said.

"No one will."

They were in each other's arms. Glenn slipped his hand under her blouse and gently fondled one of her breasts. Marie's lips danced softly and slowly around his ear. I felt queasy and wanted to get away from them, but I wanted to know what they were talking about.

"You think you can control him?" he asked.

"What do you think?"

She dropped to her knees and began to unbuckle his belt. A wave of nausea hit me, and I felt something nasty start to creep up from my gut. I couldn't take anymore. I'd seen and heard enough. I slinked back into the darkness of the hallway, trying to comprehend what I had witnessed. I could have confronted them, I suppose, but I needed to protect Isabelle as I knew this would break her heart

When I got back to my room, I sat on my bed, my head in my hands. I didn't know how to deal with what I had witnessed. Outside, I thought I heard the sound of a car driving away, but when I went to the window, I couldn't see a thing through the fog that filled the air.

Raven had once told me that everyone's family had skeletons in their closet. I thought I knew my family, but I felt like I was back on the Sea Serpent, out of control as we crashed this time into the cold water below. My father's hand reached up from the dark depths of the water and pulled me under. His mouth stuffed with seaweed, his bloated body taking me down to witness the horrible wreckage at the bottom of the ocean, wreckage that I'd never be prepared to face.

CHAPTER TWENTY-ONE

THE PALE-FACED MAN

HE SAT BACK under one of the orange trees and watched him. A cigarette would have been nice, real nice. He hated waiting and a good smoke passed the time well. The cop had parked his car off the long driveway amid a cluster of scrub oak and olive trees before walking in the shadows, through the fog, creeping up slowly and cautiously to the house. He followed the cop, but stayed well behind him. The cop had been watching the couple on the front porch. The two were kissing, and then the girl started using her mouth on the guy. The pale-faced man watched without getting aroused. He couldn't get aroused anymore. The doctors said it wasn't anything physical, but what else could it have been? He remembered being sprayed with chemicals from American choppers while on patrol in the dense jungles of Vietnam.

In Nam there was a Vietnamese girl who did all kinds of things to him, and she didn't cost much. He never tired of it. Each time he came back from a mission, he'd go back and see Sally. It wasn't her real name. He couldn't pronounce her real name. Even though he had to rent Sally by the hour, he liked her. He doubted that she liked him. Sometimes he even tried to convince himself that she really did have a thing for him and maybe he should have tried to bring her home with him. But he knew the truth. He knew his presence made people feel uncomfortable, but he paid Sally good money to like him. And she proved to be a good actress, and that was good enough for him. She got him hooked on those damn clove cigarettes. He liked the way the cigarette dangled from her lips as she took her clothes off, and how her mouth tasted when they kissed.

The woman really went down on the guy, and he seemed to be coming out of his skin, he loved it so much. The cop, though, had seen enough and ran back to his car. The pale-faced man wanted to stay and watch the couple. Even though it didn't affect him, he was still fascinated by the animal aspect of it all. He remembered watching the woman's brother, too, doing it to that hippie chick. He'd stood right in the doorway of the bedroom and they never knew he was there. He had that gift. He'd be right next to someone, and they wouldn't know he was there until they lay dying and he was the last thing they ever saw. Sometimes they died before they knew anything was wrong. He was good at his job.

Reluctantly, he climbed on his motorcycle and went after the cop. He followed the car off the canyon road to a small dirt path that led to a creek. The cop had stopped and buried his face in his hands. He worried that the cop was going to crack. Everything seemed to be under control, but the cop was the weak link. The surfer and the hippie chick were out of the picture. He'd paid some bikers a few cases of beer to scare the hippie chick, and that seemed to do the trick. But he didn't think the cop could be trusted now. *We live in a funny world*, he thought. The cop had hired him, and now he had to kill him.

He moved downwind of the cop so he could enjoy a cigarette and watch as the guy cried his eyes out. The cop wept uncontrollably. He was in no hurry to kill him. He liked to watch his victims before he killed them—a form of foreplay, he guessed. He noticed the cop had a gun in his hand now. He could see the internal struggle. The cop wanted to die; he wanted to kill himself, but he couldn't do it. He watched a while longer. The cop cradled his revolver like a teddy bear. After he finished his third cigarette, he walked silently out of the fog and to the car. He reached through the car's open window and gently took the gun from the cop. The cop turned and recognized him. "You," he mouthed. The cop appeared to be frightened, and then he seemed to relax. The cop seemed to welcome what came next. He placed the gun in the cop's hand and pushed it gently up against the roof of his mouth, and then put him out of his misery.

CHAPTER TWENTY-TWO

I DREADED SEEING MARIE, Glenn, and Isabelle at the breakfast table. I wasn't sure what I was going to do, though kicking the living shit out of Glenn was a distinct possibility. But, as I discovered, I had no reason to worry. I was the only one up. Eight on a Monday morning and I was the first one down. Graciella greeted me with coffee, *huevos rancheros*, and *The Register*.

"Where is everybody?"

Graciella shrugged. "Your mother is not feeling well. The mornings have not been kind to her lately."

I knew what she was alluding to. "Did she drink much before my dad died?"

"No, she rarely drank at all. You should talk to her."

Graciella looked at me, waiting for me to respond. When I didn't, she shook her head and went back to the sink.

Normally, I would have asked Marie to talk to my mom. She was the rock of the family, but I could no longer be confident about her judgment. I chased the image of her and Glenn from my mind, but found that my appetite had left me. Something else had been bothering me as well. Something I had been unable to ignore.

"Graciella, I want you to be honest. What did you think of my dad?"

She kept her back to me as she washed the dishes. Graciella worked six days a week for us, from before breakfast until just after dinner. She must have known things. Graciella once covered for Dawn and me when we were almost caught making love in the living room by my mother. I wondered if she knew about Marie and Glenn. I wondered what else she might have known.

"You loved your father. What I think shouldn't matter."

"Maybe I didn't know him like I thought I did, or even my family for that matter."

"Every family has secrets."

"Yes, but they shouldn't be secret from the family."

"It is not my place, Liam. But I will tell you that Mr. Felix had power, and he liked to use it. Many people feared him. Your father got what he wanted, and he did not care how he got it."

That didn't sound like him, but everything about my family was new to me, as if we had all lived in a fictional world of my own creation.

Graciella turned around to face me.

"I said too much. Your father loved you, Liam. That much I know. He was very proud of you."

"Who was scared of my father?"

Graciella said something harsh to herself in Spanish. She grabbed a sponge and started scrubbing a pan. The water must have been very hot, because a cloud of steam raced upwards from the sink.

She turned her face toward me, her jaws clenched. "Nobody wanted to say no to Mr. Felix. Not many did."

Graciella stopped for a moment and then opened her mouth as if she were about to say more. But then she threw down the sponge and stormed out of the kitchen, leaving the hot water running. The steam stained the window above the sink, obscuring my view of the world outside.

The hot mist drifted my way, but that wasn't what caused my eyes to sting. I wanted to run after her and tell her she was wrong, but it would have been pointless. I couldn't explain it, but somehow I knew she was right. What Graciella told me seemed to hurt her as much as it hurt me. The words of the cop at the beach the night they found my dad came rushing back to me.

Just how well did he know his father?

Just how well did I know my father? One time, when I was around six years old, he took me to Hudson's Dairy, a small store just off Ocean Boulevard. They sold fresh eggs, butter, soft drinks and, I thought, the best chocolate milk in the world. My dad picked up two bottles, and when the cashier gave him his change, my father counted it.

"Excuse me," my father said.

My hand gripped his tightly, wondering what he wanted from the cashier.

"Yes, sir?" the cashier replied.

"I think you gave me too much change back."

My dad handed the cashier thirteen cents.

As we walked out to the car, I couldn't believe my father would willingly give up free money. I could think of a lot of things I could buy with thirteen cents.

"Why'd you give him back the money?"

"It wasn't mine, Liam. It wouldn't have been right." He stopped and knelt down. He put his hands on my shoulders and gave me a kind look. "You understand, don't you?"

I did. At that very moment everything I thought about my dad had been confirmed. He was a good man, and I was proud to be his son. But everything since my father's murder led me back to the cop's question, taunting me:

Just how well did he know his father?

It didn't matter which of the cops had said it because it seemed to be common knowledge to the police. I wanted to talk to Dane. Maybe there were people out there who wanted my father dead. I had to know why and who would want to kill him. Then there were the black cigarettes I'd found outside of our house. I needed to convince Dane to reopen the case.

Dane was a creature of habit. When he wasn't working, he could be found at Johnny-Bob's Donuts. Being on Pacific Coast Highway made it an ideal place to girl-watch and bullshit with his old high school buddies. Dane seemed to live in an even smaller world than mine. While he wanted to be a big gun, he only wanted to be one in La Bolsa. Either he had no interest in the world outside of his hometown, or he was frightened of what lived beyond the city limits. I really couldn't knock him because I was no longer sure why I preferred the water over land. Was it purely the love of the water or a fear of all that lay on the shore and beyond?

When I had graduated from Long Beach State, I remember Dawn rushing up to me, her Kodak Instamatic in her hand. As she took my picture, she asked me a simple question.

"Hey Liam," she said, brushing her brown hair from her eyes, while I tried to set my cap just right, holding my diploma in my hand. "What are you going to do now?" I heard the click of the camera and then Dawn telling me that I forgot to smile.

"Liam, you're letting the water run." Marie shut off the faucet. "What's wrong? Do you feel okay?" The image of her with Glenn flashed back in my mind, only for a second, but that was long enough.

"I have to go."

On my way out the front door, I saw Glenn and Isabelle walking hand in hand down the stairs. They were a beautiful couple, stunning actually, and though they were smiling, they looked as if they desperately wanted to be anywhere but next to each other. They stood still for a second, frozen on the stairway. I nodded to them and shot out the front door before any one of us could say anything. As I got to my truck, I glanced through the front window. They were still frozen on the stairs, as if taking the next step down would shatter everything they had worked so hard to create.

CHAPTER TWENTY-THREE

THE MORNING FOG was still thick, but the sea air felt good on my face. I rolled down the window and let it wash over me as I drove down La Bolsa Canyon Road. I turned on KRLA and was greeted by The Who's "I Can See for Miles," which made me laugh because I could barely see ten feet in front of me. Roger Daltrey sang about how he was deceived, but because he had magic in his eyes, he knew the truth. I caught my breath.

A police car blocked a narrow stretch of the road in front of me, its lights flashing. A patrolman leaned against the top of the car with one hand. The other held the microphone that he shouted into. I stopped and got out of my truck.

"You'll have to turn around. We're going to be here for a while."

He pointed down to the gully. I recognized the car. Blood was splattered all over the windows. I wasn't going to find Dane Lohan at Johnny-Bob's, and he was in no shape to talk to me or anyone else.

The officer appeared to be fresh from the Academy, and he fought to keep his hands from shaking.

"What happened?"

"I climbed down to the vehicle and saw it up close. I'm no expert, but it looks like suicide to me. Shot himself in the head. What a mess. Jesus."

He covered his mouth and ran to the other side of the road, where I heard him retching. It must have been Dane's car that I heard driving away last night. Did he witness Marie and Glenn? Was that what caused him to pull the trigger?

The news of Dane's suicide affected Marie more than I thought it would. She had always led him on, getting what she wanted, then dismissing him at the drop of a hat. It was a game that Dane had willingly played along with. But when I told Marie the news, she put her hand to her mouth and let out an audible gasp.

"Where did you say he died?"

"Down by the creek. That bend where the road narrows."

"Where the Joshua tree is," she whispered, more to herself than to me. She glanced up, her eyes rimmed with tears.

Few people knew of the lone Joshua tree that grew down by the creek. To me, it seemed like a lost child waiting to be rescued and taken back to the desert where it belonged. "That's where he first told me that he loved me. It was his birthday. He had just turned eighteen. Dane showed me where he had carved our initials into the tree. I laughed at him. God, he was like that tree. He never knew his place. And now this."

With that, she stormed out of the room. I wondered what device had kept Marie's blood pumping through her body, because I knew it couldn't have been a heart.

CHAPTER TWENTY-FOUR

I ATTENDED THE FUNERAL services for Dane Lohan. The Santa Anas had returned, pushing the dirty air over the ocean, creating a bright, beautiful day. Though Isabelle and Glenn didn't know Dane well, Marie made sure they were present, no doubt hoping their presence at the funeral would make the local papers. Voters would like that. Marie, herself, looked magnificent in black, as if she were made for funerals. It was one of those big police affairs that drew hundreds of uniforms from all over Southern California. Since Dane was well known around town, a lot of local VIPs were there. I spotted Archibald Roth with his cowboy hat in hand, Gus Schilling, some city councilmen, the mayor. And there, lost in the crowd, I saw Bonnie Kiyan. She was alone, no mother or sister at her side. Had she known Dane? I couldn't recall ever seeing them together. I stayed in the back with a few guys from our old high school basketball team.

Dane's mother broke down when the police chief handed her the American flag that had been draped over his casket. Dane's father tried to comfort her, but then he broke, too. That's when I had to leave. As I walked back to my truck, the scent of clove cigarette smoke surrounded me and I stopped. My heart raced. He was here. I scanned the sea of mourners, but I couldn't spot him. Somehow he was able to hide himself in a crowd of uniformed police officers. I marveled at the irony. Bonnie Kiyan stared at me like she wanted to tell me something, but then quickly turned away. My mind was on the pale-faced man. I worried where he might go next. I ran to my truck and headed straight to Raven's apartment.

Raven lived off Ocean Boulevard in one of those new apartment complexes that seemed to model themselves after Disneyland. The Key West apartments, or "Floridaland" as Raven referred to them, were surrounded by palm trees, a fake shipwreck, and a few of what appeared to be beached canoes that housed tropical plants. I found it odd that apartments in the area wanted to attract renters by saying, "It's like living somewhere other than California." I was surprised there wasn't a statue of a pirate, or of Ernest Hemingway, out front greeting guests.

Raven hadn't lived here long and the fact that she'd actually paid a first and last month's rent indicated she might stay around for a while. I ran upstairs to her apartment and knocked on the door.

"Raven, it's me."

I knocked again and tried the doorknob, but it was locked. I tried looking through her window, but her curtains made that impossible. I put my ear to the door and heard the faint sounds of The Doors' "People are Strange" coming from inside. I knocked again and this time called out her name. Nothing.

I hustled down the stairs and tried to find the manager's apartment. I crossed by the swimming pool, and that's where I found her.

She was lying on her stomach on a chaise lounge by the pool. Her bikini straps were undone, exposing her back to the sun. A magazine lay open below her, the pages turned silently in the wind. Her long red hair covered her face. A lone fly buzzed above her. I searched for a sign of life and was relieved when I saw her wave her arm, attempting to chase the fly away. I studied her for a moment. For someone who lived life the way she did, she was still an innocent. Not naïve. No. She carried a wisdom about her. Innocent and wise, that was the best way to describe Raven.

I yelled out a hello. Startled, she rose and turned my way. Her bikini top slipped down off of her breasts and she brought her hands up to cover them.

"Oh." She smiled. "It's you." She dropped her hands, exposing herself to me for a moment before tying the straps of her bikini top.

"Liam, you're blushing."

I shrugged and gave her a sheepish grin.

"You are something else, Liam Sol. What are you so dressed up for?"

"Dane Lohan's funeral was this morning."

"Yeah, I heard. I didn't really know him, otherwise..."

"I know."

I sat down in the chair next to her.

"You know, you can sit a little closer."

"Last time you were close to me... if you weren't with me that night you wouldn't have—"

"Don't blame yourself."

"He's back," I said, as I watched a bee struggle in the pool water.

"Who? How do you know?"

I told her about the funeral and the cigarette smell. The color drained from her face, and she wrapped herself tightly in the towel.

"But you didn't see him?"

I told her I hadn't. "He hid himself in the crowd, but I knew it was him. He was there."

"Did you start looking into your father's murder again?"

When I didn't answer, she repeated the question.

"No. Not really. I haven't done anything, but I know he came to my parents' house as well. I saw the same cigarettes that were at my place. I think he may have been watching Marie."

"Why?"

"That's what I need to find out."

"Why would he be at Dane Lohan's funeral?"

"I don't know. To see if she was there?"

"Liam, it doesn't make any sense. Is anyone else looking into who killed your father? Was Dane?"

"I don't think so. In fact, I was going to ask him to reopen the case. Maybe he already had. Maybe he learned something."

"What?"

"I heard a car drive away from my parents' house the night he killed himself. It must have been his car, Raven."

"Liam, you're reaching for something that might not be there."

"No. Wait. The night the pale-faced guy came to my house, he mentioned something about Eddie Capuano getting killed. Not suicide. Killed. Christ. Maybe Dane didn't kill himself, either. Maybe it wasn't suicide."

"You think this guy killed your father, too."

I rubbed my face with my hands. "I don't know, but I have to find out. I'm sorry, Raven."

Her eyes found some distant and remote spot to focus on.

"What are you going to do?"

"Keep out of this guy's sight. It's not going to be easy."

Raven reached over and grabbed my hands, her palms cold and damp. "I want to help."

That was Raven for you. "No. If I start asking questions again, he might come after you. He did it once already. You need to stay far away from this. Is there anywhere you can go?"

She tried to keep her voice steady. “Some friends asked me to go up to Salinas with them.”

“You should go.”

“I’m not going anywhere.”

“Raven—”

“I don’t want to leave you alone.”

“You won’t be. I just don’t want anything to happen to you. I’m responsible for all this. When are your friends leaving?”

“Tomorrow. In the morning.”

“You need to get packing.”

Raven gripped my hand. “You’re going to be careful, right?”

I told her I would, though I had no idea what my next step would be.

I walked Raven back to her apartment and made sure she locked the door behind her. Suddenly the wind stopped, and for a moment it seemed as if the world held itself in some kind of limbo. But in the distance, the sudden sound of a car slamming its brakes was followed by the inevitable sound of metal crashing into metal. People started shouting and screaming for help, and then the winds picked up again, drowning out their screams with the low, haunting howl of the Santa Anas. The winds, it seemed, determined what was of significance, and apparently those in distress ranked low on its list of priorities.

CHAPTER TWENTY-FIVE

I SAW A NOTE under my front door when I got home. I paused before reading it. Instinctively, I scanned the yard. I caught no scent of cigarettes, but still I felt uneasy. I unfolded the paper. I didn't recognize the handwriting, but it was beautiful, bordering on the artistic. *Sorry I missed you*, the note read. *I'll be hanging out at the pier for a while if you want to meet up. Bonnie Kiyan.*

I hadn't been on that pier since the death of my father. The sun had started to set, and the thought of a trap certainly crossed my mind. But I didn't think the pale-faced guy needed to set me up. He knew where I lived, and getting into my house obviously wasn't an issue for him.

I found Bonnie at the end of the pier. She held a bottle of Hamm's beer in her hand, her eyes set on the oil drilling platforms that lit up the horizon. She must have changed her clothes after the funeral. She wore a pink T-shirt, well-worn Levi's, and thong sandals. She had never dressed anything like this at La Bolsa High. I wondered how her mother felt about her wearing such casual clothes.

Bonnie must have sensed my arrival, because she spoke to me before I could say hello.

"Don't you get sick of this place?"

She turned around and took a sip from her beer bottle. The wind pushed against her T-shirt, and it was obvious that she wasn't wearing a bra. The writing on the front of her shirt shouted, "Make Love Not War." I knew Mrs. Kiyan would not approve, but I had to admit that I liked the look. This was not the same girl I had known in high school—the prim, proper, studious girl who had kept to herself. There was a dark edge to her now. I glanced out to the horizon and focused on the quiet lights of Catalina Island. Bonnie had matured since high school and didn't seem shy about letting everyone know. She was an attractive girl who exuded sexuality and seemed to enjoy it. Yet, I sensed something unreal about her. Something I couldn't quite place, but it was there. It had nothing to do with the stupid things my mother would tell me: "You can never trust the Orientals. They act polite and talk nice, but they're a sneaky people."

It amazed me how my mother would get upset when she heard people talking about Mexicans in a derogatory way, then belt out something like that.

"I heard you came by the house a while back. You kind of upset my mom. If you need anything, just ask me first, okay? And sorry about my cousins. They can get pretty rough sometimes."

"I hope I didn't hurt them too badly."

She smiled. "I think they'll survive."

"Why'd they go after me?"

"They don't like white people too much, and we've had a few unwelcome visitors lately."

"What do you mean?" I asked.

"People dropping by and asking about our land, suggesting to us that it would be a shame if anything happened to our strawberry crop."

The Kiyans did own prime real estate. Over a hundred acres nestled in a shallow valley near the ocean. A terrific location for a housing tract, which I was sure was worth a lot of money.

"Did you call the police?"

"I talked to Dane Lohan. He told me not to worry. He'd take care of it."

"Yeah, Dane liked to say that he'd take care of things." I thought about when the pale-faced guy came to my house and threatened me. Dane encouraged me not to report it, said he'd personally look into it. Then it hit me. Dane never asked me for a description of the guy. Was it an oversight, was he too nervous to think straight, or had he already known who the guy was?

"It's funny. I always thought he was special. He used to tell me that we could have..." She folded her arms across her chest and glanced down at her feet. "Live and learn, I guess."

Yeah, live and learn, I thought. Could Dane have been a player in all this?

"I don't know if you've heard," she said, "but there's also been talk of rezoning. Basically kicking us off our land and getting it at a bargain. Apparently, you never really own anything in this world."

She took another sip of beer and glared at me.

"You know, all this shit started happening right after your father's murder."

"What does my father have to do with this?"

"He kept the wolves at bay, especially the big wolf, Archibald Roth."

I had no idea that my father and Archibald Roth had ever crossed swords.

"What did Roth want?"

"What he always wants. Everything."

"My father never asked your mother about selling the land?"

"He knew we didn't want to sell it. It's our home."

"Have you had any strange-looking visitors asking about your land?"

She held the bottle tightly in both hands, as if she were scared it might slip out of her fingers. "These guys seemed like regular businessmen. You know, Jim Anderson, *Father Knows Best* types. What about you, Liam? Why'd you come to our house that day?"

"I wanted to know why you all were at my father's funeral. You stayed so far away, it was like you were all hiding, like you were scared someone might see you."

"My mother asked us to go to the funeral with her. What is it with you?"

I sighed. "I think someone other than Eddie Capuano killed my father. And I'm having doubts that Dane Lohan killed himself. I'm trying to find out what I can."

"What do you mean?" Bonnie's voice dropped to almost a whisper.

"There's this pale-faced guy. I think he's stalking me. Maybe my family, I don't know. I'm going to find out, though. I'm going to find out who he is and what's going on."

She bit her lip and then finished her beer in one big gulp before tossing the bottle into the ocean.

"I should get back to UCLA. Dissertations are a royal bitch."

She rushed past me, her eyes avoiding contact with mine.

"Do you know something about this guy? Have you seen him?"

She glanced over her shoulder at me, and squinted as if a bright light had targeted her face.

"Stay safe, Liam. Okay?"

As Bonnie walked away, a strong gust of wind came up and tossed her long dark hair back, and I thought that it might carry her off at any second.

I watched the waves for a while, following the tide as it rolled onto shore, to the place where they'd found my father's body. I tried to put together what little I knew. I didn't even know where to start. I wasn't cut out for any of this.

Off in the distance I heard a fishing boat chugging out to sea. The crew soon would be out in darkness, alone in the middle of the ocean. A chill settled in my bones, as if warning me that something dangerous was near. I scanned the area, but saw no one else on the pier. There was no hint of clove cigarette smoke in the air, but still I felt a presence watching me. It filled the air around me, and something primal in me urged me to flee. I felt vulnerable and scared. I started to walk back. My strides got longer, my pace quicker, and I finally broke out into a full sprint, until I found myself on solid ground.

That night, I put the leather chair against my front door. I knew it wouldn't do much to keep me any safer, but still it was something. Eventually, I fell asleep on my couch while watching Johnny Carson. I woke up at two in the morning to the national anthem. A jet fighter raced across the TV screen, protecting America, I guessed, from all enemies. I turned the set off and walked into the kitchen. I opened a bottle of Coors and watched the oil wells from my kitchen window slowly pump out the crude. Soon the wells would dry up, and the land would be converted into a brand-new housing development.

What the hell had Dane been up to? He keeps an eye on Marie, and tells both Bonnie and me that he'll take care of our situations. Then he winds up dead. I was going to have to talk to the police, but that would be an advertisement to the pale-faced guy that I was back snooping around. He was still out there, and I was sure he'd kill me if he found out what I was up to. He'd probably make it look like a suicide, too. I needed to keep out of his sight for as long as possible, but I knew it was only a matter of time before he found out. He was the key to learning the truth. I knew that. But who was he? Why was he in the picture? Had he been threatening the Kiyans? I felt my entire body tense up, and my heart, I was sure, had just skipped a few beats. I finished my beer and then pulled the rest of the six-pack out of the fridge. I sat back on the couch, looking out the window, drinking beer, and listening to the crash of the waves until I finally fell asleep, just as the sun began to rise.

CHAPTER TWENTY-SIX

My parents' house was a storm of activity. Workers set up folding chairs in the living room while maids I'd never seen before arranged and placed flowers—all under the direction of Marie, who stomped around with a large vase in her hand.

"You don't plan on staying long, do you?"

"Marie—"

"Liam, give me a break. You look like you're hungover, and we're hosting a big fundraiser for Glenn tonight. You're not exactly the image we'd like to portray."

Marie was right. I knew I looked like shit. I felt like someone had shoved cotton down my throat and was now trying to crush my skull, but I didn't want to let Marie off so easily.

"There will be food tonight, right?"

"Liam, so help me God..."

I wanted to volunteer to represent the drunken surfer vote. But she had that vase in her hand, and Marie had a quick temper and little humor.

"Relax, these are the last people I'd want to be seen with. I have an image to maintain, too, you know."

I climbed the stairs and made my way to my father's office. The door to Glenn and Isabelle's room was open, and I saw Glenn, standing naked except for his jockey shorts, in front of the mirror, practicing his speech. He had his gut sucked in, and he tried to find the right tone for his voice: "Together we can make La Bolsa a modern city, a guiding light for all who dream of building a city, not only for this century, but for the twenty-first as well." He put his hands up as if he were trying to quiet the inevitable applause that would follow. I kept moving. I'd seen enough of Glenn with his pants down to last a lifetime.

My father had liked to keep the business simple. There were never a lot of people involved. No big staff. Most of the office work he was able to do at home. He didn't have a building or a team of flunkies working for him. He had one secretary, Jane Bithell, who had retired a few years ago. Since then, Marie had seemed to take on the role of secretary and advisor to my father. He bought up the available land he wanted, determined what to build, and then partnered with Archibald Roth to get the job done.

I hadn't thought about Jane Bithell in a long time. Growing up, she always seemed so modern. The way she wore bright-colored scarves over her hair reminded me of Grace Kelly in *To Catch a Thief*. An image came to me from long ago. I must have been ten years old. Her red MG parked in our driveway. My mother, Marie, and Isabelle were in San Francisco to visit my Aunt Eileen. It was an early Monday morning, the sun had just started to rise, and I was waiting, surfboard by my side, for Hike's brother to pick me up. A bunch of dried leaves rested on the hood of her car, as if it had been parked there overnight, but I hadn't noticed the car in the driveway until just then. I studied the red car for a moment and tried not to put the pieces together. Then I heard the rumble of Hike's brother's 1940 Ford Woody approaching, and any thoughts I might have had fled as we headed out to Rincon. Until now,

I hadn't thought about her red MG parked in our driveway while my mother was away.

Why that thought found its way to me now, I didn't know. But as I walked into my father's office, I realized there must've been something going on between him and Jane that, as a child, I couldn't have known. I was too innocent, too trusting. The realization that he had cheated on my mom made my stomach turn, as if I had swallowed something rancid.

I glanced around the office, but I had no idea what I wanted to find. A note from my father saying, "In case of my murder, here's the name of the person who did it," was probably too much to ask for. Marie was using his office now as well, so I didn't know what was what. I glanced at the pictures on his desk. I saw one of me at the beach, sitting on my father's shoulders, both our eyes bright while the sun set behind us. He appeared to be as proud of me as I was of him. Something was missing among the pictures, though. I realized there were no pictures of Isabelle. I knew there had been. One when she must have been ten, reading a Nancy Drew book to my father, her eyes wide, a finger waving in the air, as she acted out the scene for him. There was another one, too, I was sure, but I couldn't recall the image. Isabelle must have wanted them for herself. I examined the picture of my dad when he was a child. He tried to stand tall next to my grandfather, Jesus. The photo had cracked with age, but I could tell it had been taken in front of the house. The orange groves that surrounded the house were just tiny saplings. A trace of a gleam in my grandfather's eyes stood out, as if declaring, "I told you so." I studied the set of *Encyclopedia Americana* and smiled. I always loved hearing the legendary family story of the encyclopedias that started it all.

My grandfather worked as a sugar beet harvester in Oxnard just past the turn of the century. He was new to America, and it was the only job he could find. The work was hard, and the bosses treated them all like shit. Jesus took part in the first agricultural strike in California.

The result was more pay, but still barely enough to live on. And the work got harder as the landowners made them suffer for even daring to launch a strike.

According to my grandfather, a slick man in a fancy suit came by one day and offered a free parcel of land in a place called La Bolsa to anyone who bought a set of encyclopedias from him. Jesus bought two sets, one for home and one for the local school. Education, he believed was the only way out for his children. He convinced his brother and a number of friends to invest as well. They were resistant at first, but my grandfather talked them into it. The promise of being real landowners appealed to them all.

My grandfather and a couple of his friends took a few days off and traveled down to La Bolsa to check on the land. It wasn't what any of them had pictured. You couldn't live on this land. It consisted of marshes and mosquitoes. My grandfather's friends berated him for talking them into this. They didn't want the encyclopedias. They wanted land, a place where they could build a home and call their own.

My grandfather felt responsible, and against the protests of my grandmother, he bought back each set of encyclopedias along with the accompanying land. It took him three years, but he did it. Still, neither his friends nor his brother ever let him forget what an idiot they thought he was.

One summer evening after a brutal day's work, Jesus was drinking in a local cantina when a fancy car pulled up and out stepped the encyclopedia salesman. Jesus walked out and greeted him with a punch in the jaw, knocking him out. When the salesman regained consciousness, he told my grandfather that oil had been discovered on his land and on every parcel he'd bought back from his brother and friends.

His first instinct was to share the wealth, but my grandmother reminded him of how poorly everyone had treated him. Rather than letting everyone know about their newly found wealth, they snuck out in the middle of the night and never looked back.

After he retired, my grandfather turned the business over to my dad. The oil poured in for years, but eventually some of the wells began to dry up. My grandparents lived long enough to watch with pride as my father plowed over the empty oil wells, filled in the marshes, and built profitable housing tracts.

There were many ways to achieve the American dream, my grandfather would say—he just never imagined that a set of encyclopedias could do so much for a man's future.

I sat at my father's desk and examined Marie's notepad. She had written down various names and numbers that I didn't recognize. I flipped through the pages and stopped when I came across the page with "Kiyan" on it. Just like the note that had sent me to their farm back in September. Why had Marie written their name down as well?

Bonnie had mentioned that things got worse for them after my father died. I could go to Marie and ask, but I had to admit to myself that I didn't trust her. Jesus Christ, I didn't trust my own sister.

I went through the other notes until I found one in my father's handwriting. What I saw made me freeze. No name had been written down, but I recognized the number. It was Dawn's, and next to it, her home address. A sick feeling washed over me. Why had he called her? Or had she called him?

I flipped through the rest of the notes, but I didn't find anything of interest. I scanned the office and noticed the small filing cabinet.

I went through the file drawers and searched under K for the Kiyans. Nothing. I looked under L for Lohan, nothing. I also checked for Arnett, but as I expected, nothing about Dawn. I slammed the drawer shut and sat back in the chair.

What did Dawn have to do with my dad? The image of Jane Bithell's red MG in the driveway flashed in my mind. No. It wasn't that. No, it had to be something else. But what?

I didn't see anything more in my father's office to look through. I didn't know how he went about his business, but still found it hard to believe that he kept so few records. I had nothing more to go on, except to talk to Dawn and find out what she had been doing with my father. Horrible images of the two of them jumped into my mind, and I couldn't push them away. It wasn't rational. I knew that. But still they came to me in a rapid slide show.

As I walked out of the office, I bumped into Glenn. He wore a navy blue suit with a red tie. He appeared to be the perfect citizen, upstanding and respectable, like someone you'd trust to hold on to your wallet and keep it safe. My father had liked to say that the suit makes the man. Well, a suit could also disguise who that man really was.

"Hey, Liam, are you staying for the reception? We'd love to have you," Glenn said.

He was all smiles. Everything was right in his world. And why not? He marries into a wealthy family and gets to fuck both sisters under the same roof.

He tried to step by me, but I blocked his path. A rage had been building inside of me. I didn't like the feeling. It felt as if I were no longer in control of myself, as if some foreign entity had taken over. I tried to keep my emotions in check, but they were slipping away fast.

"Everything okay?" he asked.

The world got fuzzy for a second. Glenn went in and out of focus. And then suddenly his face became too clear, and it was the only thing I could see. I grabbed his tie and pushed him into the wall. He let out a gasp, and his eyes grew wide.

I liked that I hurt him. He was frightened of me, and it made me feel good.

"Stay away from Marie."

I could see that he tried to figure out what I meant, what I knew, and why I was so angry.

"She's my campaign manager."

"You know what I mean, you little shit. Just keep your fucking pants zipped up around her. You're married to Isabelle. Isabelle, not Marie."

"You don't understand."

"Goddammit. There's nothing to understand."

I pulled his tie harder and brought his face to less than an inch from mine. I could smell the Listerine on his breath. It made me feel sick to my stomach. I was out of control, and it scared the hell out of me.

I grabbed his face with my other hand and slammed his head into the wall. "You know. You know what I'm saying. If you hurt Isabelle, I'll… no more. You got that? No more."

I let go of him. He stayed frozen against the wall. I pointed my finger at him and then walked away.

"You don't know shit, Liam." His voice cracked. "You have no idea what's going on."

My rage didn't let up. I was tempted to go back and kick the living shit out of him and toss him off the pier. Marie stood at the bottom of the stairs, glaring at me.

"What's going on? Is Glenn all right? I heard him yelling."

I walked right past her. "He's fine." I stopped when I got to the front door and turned around. Glenn stood at the top of the stairs, adjusting his suit. Marie's mouth parted slightly as if she were trying to find the right words to calm me, but she knew there was nothing she could say. Isabelle walked up to Glenn and helped him with his tie. Her eyes found mine, and I could see the tears begin to fall. I mouthed, "I'm sorry," to her and walked out.

I sat in my truck for a moment, trying to take it all in, wondering if

Isabelle knew what had been going on between her husband and Marie? Or did my outburst give it all away? I examined the house I had grown up in, and I knew it held more secrets than I could ever imagine.

I parked on a bluff that overlooked Puente Bay. I sat on the hood of my truck. The winds were blowing strong, and I could see a thin trail of dark smoke rising from the hillsides to the south. Another fire rearing up; this one looked to be a good distance from our house.

I stared at the ocean. I was tempted to climb down and take a long swim in its cool waters. But I knew I was stalling. I knew that I had to visit Dawn. I knew I had to ask her what had been going on with her and my father. I knew, too, that seeing her was the last thing I was prepared to do.

Everything in my life was turning out to be a far cry from what I had once thought. The Beach Boys were singing "When I Grow Up To Be a Man" on my car radio. I smiled. I couldn't help it. Despite—or because of—the circumstances in which I found myself, the irony was not lost on me. I had been living life with my eyes shut. Some of my fellow surfers in La Bolsa weren't the nicest people in the world. They didn't drive around in little deuce coupes being true to their school. Many of the younger surfers had taken on a harder edge, seemingly always looking for fights, an anger building inside them that they were unable to comprehend or conceal. No, Frankie and Annette never lived here, Gidget left for Paris, Jan Berry crashed near Dead Man's Curve, and Brian Wilson was on acid. Part of me wished the winds would push this new fire all the way to La Bolsa and take everything with it.

My encounter with Glenn left me exhausted. I didn't know I had that in me, and I didn't feel good about it. I was no hippie, but I had no clue that I could go ape like that on anyone. It's not that I cared a lick about Glenn. I'd never liked the guy, but why did I have to explode on him when Isabelle was around? I wasn't looking forward to facing my family; they were more trouble than they were worth. I was tempted to take up Hike's and Lonnie's invitation to go on another surf trip to Mexico. It wasn't too late. They were heading out early tomorrow. I could get drunk, chase women, and leave my family far behind, maybe for good this time. Hell, maybe I'd go to Westwood and hit up on Bonnie Kiyan. It all sounded good, damn good, but I knew I couldn't do it. Maybe I wasn't that person anymore.

CHAPTER TWENTY-SEVEN

I DROVE TO DAWN'S house. Her VW Bug was parked out front, so I pulled up in her driveway. I stayed in the truck, not wanting to move. I was nervous as hell about seeing her. I hadn't spoken to her in a long time. I missed her in my life. I missed the way she made me feel, but she and my father had been involved in something—something that could have been related to his murder.

I tried to look through her front window. Then the curtains moved, and I saw Dawn's face peek out, her eyes locked on mine. I gripped the steering wheel, and my legs felt as if they were nailed to the floor of the truck.

She came out of the house, the sun shining brightly on her face. She wore a white Mexican peasant blouse and cut-off Levi's that showed off her deeply tanned legs. The wind tossed her dark hair in front of her face, and she tried to put it back behind her ears.

"Are you stuck to the steering wheel?"

"I think I might be."

She walked up to the truck, putting her hands into her pockets.

"I can call the fire department. They get cats out of trees. I'm sure they can get old boyfriends out of trucks."

Old boyfriends. She stopped inches from the truck, shook her head, and then came up next to me and rested her arms on the open window. When she leaned through the window, a hint of cleavage peeked out from the top of her blouse, just enough to make me steal a glance. Just enough for me to remember.

"I have to apologize," she said. "I've been meaning to come over since your father died, but..." Her voice trailed off.

"But?"

"I don't know, Liam. I actually drove by your place a few times. I just couldn't bring myself to knock on your door."

I knew what she felt. It took everything I had and then some just to get to her driveway.

"So, what brings you here?"

"My father. I need to talk to you about him."

She asked me if I wanted to come inside the house. I pictured the two of us after I had helped her move in. Laughing, holding each other, and me whispering promises to her that I was incapable of keeping. When I didn't answer, she walked over to the other side of the truck, opened the door, and sat in the passenger seat.

"Let's go to Rosa's. I could use a cold beer," she said.

The drive to Rosa's took much longer than it should have. Traffic was bumper to bumper. Up ahead I could see the flashing lights of police cars and an ambulance. An overturned station wagon, and another car that was so smashed up I couldn't recognize its make or model, blocked the highway. Pieces of metal scattered on the asphalt, as if dropped there by a sudden storm. Neither the police nor the firemen seemed to be in any hurry. That was never a good sign. My mother would make the sign of the cross and say a silent prayer whenever we heard a siren or saw an accident. I found myself doing just that, but more out of habit than anything else.

It didn't look like we'd be moving anytime soon. I cut through a vacant lot that eventually dumped out onto Ocean Boulevard. The owners of the land would let people sell their boats on the lot in the spring and summer with a big sign that read, "Sale Boats." I never knew if the spelling was intentional or not. We rode without saying a word. The familiar scent of plumeria filled the cab and covered me like a silk sheet. Dawn picked up the perfume whenever she went to Kauai. I felt my defenses breaking down. I tried to find a good song on the radio, something to distract me, but nothing could break the silence. It wasn't a calm quiet. I felt as if we both wanted to talk, but were unable or unwilling to find the right words.

Walking into Rosa's was like entering a tomb with an ocean view. The windows were open to the sun reflecting off the water, and except for the hostess and a couple of guys tossing back beers at the bar, we were alone.

"It's just one of those days," the waitress said, her voice slurred. I asked her where all the customers were. "I haven't got a clue," she replied.

"Two Dos Equis when you get the chance," I said. I was tempted to buy the waitress a cup of coffee, but I thought she'd just pour whiskey into it.

I'd never seen Rosa's this quiet. We made our way to the opposite end of the restaurant and sat in a corner booth. The seats were warm, as if someone had been sitting there before us for a long time. Their presence, whoever they were, still seemed to be with us.

The waitress brought us our beers and asked if we wanted to order any food.

"No, just drinking today," I told her.

"Join the club," she slurred as she stumbled away.

Dawn and I shared a look, but still neither of us said a word, the awkwardness intensifying. Finally, Dawn cut the silence open with a knife.

"So, what do you want to know?"

I avoided her eyes, scared of what would come next.

"Know?"

"You said you wanted to talk to me about your father?"

Her eyes were sharp and focused on mine.

"I don't know how to ask this."

"Just ask."

"I was poking around in his office. I didn't even know what I thought I'd find. On his desk, I saw that he wrote down your phone number and your address on a notepad. It didn't make any sense. I wanted to know why." Her face reddened and she looked away.

"Why were you going through his things?"

Too many thoughts and images rushed through my mind.

"Just tell me what was going on."

"This is embarrassing, Liam." She took a sip of her beer. "He asked if there was any chance of us getting back together."

I laughed. It was involuntary, but along with the laugh, I felt my heart stop for a brief moment.

"I told you it was embarrassing."

"Why would he do that?"

"He was worried about you."

"Why?"

"He thought you were wasting your life surfing. He said you were capable of doing great things, but that you were too scared to fly out of the nest."

I recalled his words at the Beach Club: *You need to quit running away from life.* It hurt like a kick to the gut. I closed my eyes. "Did he say anything else?"

"He said that I was a good influence on you." Dawn gave me a slight smile. "I was, you know."

The kicks kept on coming. "I know."

"He loved you, Liam."

"I know. We had lunch, and he told me he wanted me to work for him," I said.

"He asked me about that. I said I didn't think you'd be interested."

"I told him that I didn't want to be like him. And then before I can take it back, he gets killed. Can you believe that?" I took a long drink of my beer. "I don't know what I want to do. I keep thinking it will come to me, but it never does."

"It's not something that comes to you, Liam. It's something you have to go after. And even then, even knowing that you might lose, you have to be willing to fight to get it."

Now, it felt as if someone had made a voodoo doll of me, and they were taking turns jabbing my heart. The walls of the restaurant felt like they were closing in on me.

"I don't like that I disappointed him."

"He was proud of you. He just wanted you to get on with your life. I told him I had faith in you. It just always takes you longer, that's all."

I wondered how long it would take and if I would know it if I saw it. I studied the bottle of Dos Equis, and for a moment I thought of the two of us in Mexico and how I'd let her go.

"When my dad asked you if we had any chance of getting back together, what did you tell him?"

"Liam."

"You were good for me, Dawn. I wanted to be a better person when I was with you. Hell, I was a better person when I was with you. And I liked that person. I liked him better than this one, anyway."

"Liam, things are different now."

"Do you love him?"

"Brian? This isn't about him."

So, that was his name. I thought about mentioning that I had seen him with Archibald Roth at the DMZ, but this wasn't the time.

"Do you love him? Do you love him more than you loved me?"

Dawn shook her head. "I can't go there with you again. You hurt me, Liam."

"I was scared. I didn't know what I was doing."

A wave crashed on the beach, the vibrations echoing throughout the restaurant. Until now, I hadn't realized that I had been hiding from the truth, but I couldn't hide it from myself any longer: I wanted her back. I wanted to fall into her arms and stay there forever. I looked into her eyes, hoping to see her heart open up, but all I saw was pain.

"I poured my soul out to you, Liam. Christ, our last weekend in Mexico, when I told you I might be pregnant, you should have seen your face. You were like Ebenezer Scrooge when he saw the ghost of Christmas future."

"But you weren't pregnant," I said, knowing that I sounded like a jackass.

"I thought I was. Even when I learned that I wasn't, you acted differently around me. You weren't the same. You were like a stranger."

"What do you mean? I was there with you."

"Yes, you were there, but you weren't *there* for me. Emotionally, you were in never-never land."

"You're the one who broke it off."

"Yes, I did. I needed to know what I meant to you. You barely put up a fight. You faked it, really. And then a few days later, I see you and Raven Andrews making out on the pier."

"Nothing happened. After a few kisses, I had to stop. I told her I still loved you. And I did."

Dawn blinked her eyes a few times, then she took in a deep breath.

"There's no going back, Liam," she said. "It won't work."

Her words hit me like a hard slap to the face. My emotions bled out of me like a bad cut. I couldn't look at her. Instead, my eyes focused on a particular groove that had been carved into the table. A tear ran down my face. And then another. They kept falling until I couldn't count them anymore. I saw that Dawn was crying now, too.

I grabbed a napkin and handed it to her, and then I took one for me and wiped my face. We glanced at each other and laughed at the image of the two us literally crying into our beers.

"Your father was right, you know."

"How do you mean?"

"He said you were capable of doing great things." She took my hand and gently squeezed it. "He was right. I wish you could see that, Liam."

I wished I could, too. Because right now all I could see was my cowardice, my mistakes, my failures, and how I had let her down the one time that she needed me the most.

"I should probably get back now," she said.

Darkness had fallen, and we headed out of the restaurant. Cars poured into the parking lot as if they had all waited for us to leave. We drove to her house in silence. As I pulled up into her driveway, I thought she'd open the door and rush inside. But instead, for some reason, Dawn sat with me in the car. And I was grateful for that. I didn't want her to leave me right now, because I thought that if she did, it would be for good.

"Why did you love me?" I asked.

She turned to me. "Liam—"

"I need to know, okay. I need to know."

She took a glimpse out the window and into the dark night. "You made me strong. Whenever I was scared of anything, anything, you always told me that I could do it."

"You can, Dawn. You can do anything."

She shook her head. "After you taught me how to surf, when I got good, you said I was ready to ride the big waves. I didn't think I was.

I was terrified to go into the lineup. None of those guys wanted me out there. I saw what they did to the others who messed up, especially the girls—the things they said to them and how they were treated."

I knew what she was saying. The boys could get pretty nasty to many of the girls who tried to ride with them. For all of the waterman talk and being one with nature, girls, even if they were as good as Joyce Hoffman or Margo Oberg, weren't always welcome in the lineup. Girls were there to look pretty and to work on their tans, and they could only stand by their man when he was done surfing.

"And you told me I was ready, that it was my time, and if they didn't like it, too fucking bad. We paddled out together, and I was so relieved that you were with me. I remember taking my place in the lineup. The looks they gave me, horrible." She closed her eyes as if reliving the moment. "And when it came to be my turn, you made sure no one dropped in on me."

"I remember the wave. You rode it as if it were made for you."

"Those guys were pissed," she said with a smile.

"They were impressed."

"I heard you yelling out behind me like a cheerleader: 'Go, Dawn, Go!'"

"They always welcomed you in the lineup after that, whether I was there or not."

Dawn shrugged. "Not exactly welcomed. I heard a lot of shit from them, but they didn't try to stop me." She paused. "Whenever I was nervous or scared of something, anything, you always said that I was ready to ride the big waves. Whenever you said those words, no matter what I had to face, I knew I could do it."

I put my hand on hers, but she pulled it away.

"It was you, Liam. You were the one who gave me the strength. I couldn't have been me without you. But you weren't able to give yourself to me. Not all of you. Not the part I needed you to give me."

"What do you mean?"

"You never let me in. You put up fences. I could see through them, but I could never climb over them."

I didn't know why she wanted that part of me, but I knew why I hadn't let her in. I was worried she'd see that I wasn't the man she thought I was, or who she wanted me to be. I was terrified that if she ever saw me, truly saw me, she'd run away.

She wiped her eyes. "You made me laugh. You made me happy. And finally, finally, you made me cry."

My body shuddered. I wanted to take everything back. I wanted to take the past and burn it and watch the ashes blow into the wind. "Dawn..."

She bit her lip, and then she held my face in her hands and kissed me, holding nothing back. The kiss lasted until we could no longer breathe. Then she wrapped her arms around me and held me like she once did—with her heart and her soul and all of her being.

"Good-bye, Liam," she whispered.

She let go of me and ran into her house. I took in a deep breath, inhaling the scent of her perfume. I could taste the salt from one of her tears that had fallen onto my lips. I kept the window rolled up so I could keep the plumeria and the taste of her tears with me for a little longer, just a little longer, before they could evaporate into the night.

I saw the lights of the pier ahead of me as I drove toward home from her house. Dawn had said good-bye as if it were forever. I don't know, maybe I was fooling myself. God knows I was good at that, but I thought I'd felt something more in that kiss, something that held a promise that this time I wasn't going to break. I recalled her words: *It's not something that comes to you, Liam. It's something you have to go after. And even then, even knowing you might lose, you have to be willing to fight to get it.*

Maybe she wasn't talking about us. It didn't matter. I wanted her back, and I wasn't going to run away this time. I'd be there for her, with all my faults, fears, and sins. I'd be there. I thought about turning the truck around and going back to her house, but it wouldn't happen overnight. Maybe it would never happen, but I had tomorrow, and the next day, and the days that followed to fight for her, to show her, and to show me, what I was made of. It was my turn to ride the big waves. And maybe, just maybe, she'd cheer me on.

CHAPTER TWENTY-EIGHT

THE PALE-FACED MAN

He stood in the doorway of her home and took it all in. A tropical scent of some kind filled the air. The girl lived in the small cottage. There were stacks of books and records everywhere. There were framed paintings on the wall of beach landscapes, but not the kind he usually saw in tourist shops. These were different. They were stark, lonely, but also held a beauty that unsettled him. He walked down the hallway and into her bedroom. Two surfboards rested against one of the walls. He examined the old weather-beaten dresser. The surfboards, the furniture, how the place felt to him—this was no girly house.

A small, framed pencil-and-ink drawing stood on top of the dresser. He wondered if she had drawn it. It was of the surfer, and he looked lost and alone. *You have no idea, surfer boy,* he thought. *You have no idea what's coming—how lost and alone you'll be.*

He opened the drawers to her dresser. Nothing but clothes. He went through each drawer and discovered that one of them held her diaries. He pulled the top one out. Then he sat on her bed and thumbed through it before stopping to read the last entry:

I saw him at his father's funeral. He looked so sad, so alone. I wanted to hold him in my arms. I wanted to take the pain from him. I wanted to... who am I kidding? I wanted him. I'll always want him. Despite it all, I still love him. God, Liam, wake up. You walk through life as if it will never end. As if nothing matters. And though you don't realize it, you act as if you don't matter. You do! If you only could see yourself through my eyes... maybe you can and that's what scares you.

After the funeral, I broke up with Brian. He'd asked me to move in with him. I can't see a future with him. Yet, I still pretend I can have one with Liam. But I have to face it: I'm lying to myself. It's a pretty lie, a beautiful lie, but it's still a lie.

I'm going to take that teaching job in La Jolla. It's lovely there—a perfect place for a new beginning.

The pale-faced man quit reading. He carefully tore the page out of the diary and placed it in his pocket. He shut the diary and put it back where he had found it. He knew killing the girl would hurt the surfer more than he'd ever been hurt. He needed to make the surfer pay.

He didn't like him. Spoiled little shit, just living an easy life, not having to work for anything, and he never had to pay the price for anything, either. The guy got by on his looks and charm—and his daddy's money. Worst of all, he didn't listen. The surfer boy hadn't listened when he told him to back off. Maybe he should have taken care of the hippie chick. He never liked giving threats—action worked better than words. Action produced consequences. People understood consequences. No one listened to him now. No one. He warned them, and they just kept on as if his words meant nothing. You couldn't just get away with that. You had to pay. Everyone had to pay. He needed to make him suffer.

The pale-faced man knew he was crossing the line. He felt he was losing control. He was good at following orders, but now that the cop was dead, he could make his own plans—and that excited him, because even he didn't know just how far he'd go in order to make people listen.

He heard a car pull up in the driveway. He walked out to the living room and peeked out the window. The two were kissing. *The last kiss*, he thought. Then the girl pulled away, and with tears falling down her face, she walked up the steps to her house.

The pale-faced man found a place to wait. Next to him, sitting on the bookcase, was the same picture he had seen in the surfer's house: the picture of the surfer with the girl. The same damn picture. He peered into her eyes until he had to turn the picture away from him. Then he heard her turn the key and open the door.

CHAPTER TWENTY-NINE

It sounded like someone was pounding the house with hammers. I sat up in bed and realized the hammers were only part of a dream, but someone was beating on my front door. The sun was barely up, and the house already felt hot. The day was going to be brutal.

I threw on my Levi's and walked to the living room. I heard a flurry of movement outside. I stopped.

"Who's there?"

"Police! Open up!"

I ran to the side window. Lined up in front of the house, I saw four police cars, their lights flashing, and about a dozen cops. Something's happened. Maybe they found out something about my father. Maybe they found the pale-faced guy. I gave them a wave through the window and ran to the front door.

I pushed the leather chair out of the way and opened the door. Then they were on me, shoving my face against the wall and pinning my arms behind me. I caught whiffs of coffee breath battling stale tobacco for air space. Out of the corner of my eye, I saw gun barrels pointed at me.

"Spread your legs. Hands behind your head!"

"Let go of my arms, so I can—"

"Don't say a word."

One of the cops relaxed his grip on me, allowing me to place my hands behind my head. One of the other cop's hands climbed up my legs and then up to my shoulders. One of them pulled my arms behind my back and I felt cold steel around my wrists, followed by the sound of the handcuffs locking. They turned me around. The house was filled with cops. The guy with the coffee breath started talking to me about my right to remain silent. I knew it wasn't a dream, but it didn't seem real either. I felt like I was trapped in a drug-induced episode of *Dragnet.*

"I think you've made a mistake."

"Are you Liam Sol?" Coffee Breath asked.

"Yes, but—"

"Then there's no mistake."

Glenn, that asshole, must have called the police on me. I looked at the cops, and I didn't know any of them, though a few faces seemed familiar.

"I didn't hurt—"

Coffee Breath got in my face. I thought he wanted to bite my nose off.

"Didn't hurt her? You wouldn't be able to recognize her. She may not make it."

Her? Raven. The pale-faced guy got to Raven. My mouth went dry. It was hard to swallow or breathe.

Coffee Breath pushed me backwards until I fell into my leather chair.

"Stay," he commanded as if talking to a dog. Then he dropped a document on my lap. "It's a warrant. We'll try to be more delicate than you were last night."

"What are you talking about? I didn't do anything!"

They all ignored me. They swarmed my kitchen, my bedroom, even the bathroom. It sounded like they were looting my house. Attila the Hun must have had more grace than these guys.

"Just let me know what you want! You don't have to wreck the place!"

I closed my eyes and said a prayer for Raven. I fought off the waves of nausea that threatened to overtake me. What had I done that had caused that pale-faced psycho to go after her? Why didn't he come after me? Killing me would have ended it all for him. There would be no one left to question anything. "Please God, let Raven be okay. Please," I whispered.

"Hey, look what we found." I opened my eyes. Coffee Breath held a shirt by his fingertips. The same shirt I'd worn last night, but it was covered with what appeared to be bloodstains. He was here. The pale-faced man had been in my home. "You're in a shitload of trouble."

After taking my fingerprints and booking me, two policemen led me in handcuffs to a small room. This was a different room than the one I had been in with Eddie Capuano. It had a different feeling as well. This was a room where prisoners were expected to confess. Inside sat a battered metal table and three folding chairs that looked like they'd been slammed against the wall a few times. A policeman stayed with me in the room. He didn't say a word, didn't even look at me. I glanced around the room, which smelled like it had been showered with ammonia. I'd seen rooms like this on TV. The walls were dull and tobacco-stained. I noticed a few spots on the ceiling indicating a leaky roof.

The door swung open and Coffee Breath and a younger detective entered. I recognized the younger guy from the beach when they found my father. He held a can of Coke in his hand.

"I'm Detective Branch," Coffee Breath said. "And this is Detective Greene."

"What's going on?" I asked.

Greene placed the Coke on the table in front of me. He popped the top and pulled a straw out of his pocket and placed it in the can. "I'm sure you're thirsty. This room makes everyone thirsty." He walked away and stood by the door, his arms folded across his chest. Branch took a seat next to me. He exhaled. I could still smell his breath. I doubted I'd ever want another cup of coffee again in my life.

"Quite a mess you made last night," he said. "How long have you known Miss Arnett?"

My stomach dropped. "Dawn? This is about Dawn?" I couldn't believe it. "Is she okay? I saw her last night and—"

"So, you admit you were with her?"

"Yes. Now, answer me, is she okay?"

"You should know. What'd you use, a baseball bat?"

I went cold. "What the hell are you talking about?"

Branch glanced over at Greene. "He's pretty good." Then he turned back to me. "Dawn Arnett. Pretty girl. Well, she was until you got a hold of her. She's in bad shape. Real bad shape. Doctors don't know if she's going to make it. You might be looking at a murder charge."

"It wasn't me. I didn't do it. You have to believe me."

"It had to be you, Sol," Branch said. "This was no robbery attempt. Nothing was taken. No, sir. This attack was deliberate. A beating like this, it's personal. It's always personal. You two were a couple once, weren't you? That's what we hear. We heard she broke your heart. What happened last night? You wanted her back and she said no? Things got out of hand. You didn't mean to hurt her. Tell us, Sol. Maybe we can work something out. You'll feel better. They always do."

I opened my mouth, but nothing came out. The bile in my stomach started to rise.

"I want to call a lawyer."

"Christ. Just come out with it, will you?"

The room started moving, the floor rising. I looked at Branch and tried to respond, but instead of speaking, the entire contents of my stomach blew out all over him.

I'd never been in a jail cell before. The smell of ammonia lingered throughout the station, but it seemed to be emanating from my cell, as if someone had tried to wash away a rotting corpse. I sat on the cot, my back against the wall. My blanket was dotted with stains from God knows what. The walls had been tattooed with scribbles, people's names, numbers, and declarations of injustice. Some of the names I recognized, and I was sure this had served as a second home to many of them. I read a few bad poems and saw some promising artwork, though a few of the artists didn't seem to know much about human anatomy. They'd put me in a cell by myself, which was a good thing as my stomach was blowing out everything but my vital organs. I had nothing left to give, just the dry heaves that kept demanding more from me.

I couldn't take my mind off what they'd told me, nor could I shake the images that found their way into my brain. Dawn savagely beaten. The bloody shirt they found. It didn't seem real. They claimed it was Dawn's blood. The pale-faced guy was behind this. He'd already proven he could get into my house anytime he wanted. But why Dawn? Why her? I shut my eyes and prayed. *Please, God. Let her be okay.*

About an hour later, the bailiff came by. I recognized him from somewhere, but I couldn't place it. He appeared to be around my age, and skinny, as if he were allergic to food. His face was round and scarred by acne.

"Come on, you can use the phone."

He opened the cell door, and I followed him to a pay phone at the end of the hall. The jail housed only four cells. Two were empty, but one held a couple of Hells Angels. They eyed me like they wanted me for dessert. I felt like a zebra being stalked by lions.

"Here you go," the bailiff said.

"You guys took my money."

"You don't need money. Just make your damn phone call, asshole."

He sauntered to his desk and picked up a *Playboy* magazine, thumbing through the pictures until he found one he settled on.

I didn't know any lawyers. My dad had used a couple of guys, but I didn't know their names. There was only one person I thought could help me.

"Hello?" Glenn answered. I heard a party going on around him, probably another campaign fundraising event. Why in the world did he have to answer the phone? I didn't want to scare my mom, and Isabelle wasn't equipped for this. Marie knew how to get things done. I hated myself for needing her.

"Is Marie there?"

"Is that you, Liam? You know, if you weren't Isabelle's brother—"

Yeah, and if you weren't the biggest piece of living shit in the world, I thought. "Save it, Glenn. Can you get her for me?"

"Well, she's kind of busy right now. I'd be happy to take a message for her."

"Put her on the goddamned phone. This is an emergency."

"I'll see if I can find her." He said it like he was in no rush to get her.

I examined the writings on the wall. They were similar to the ones in my cell: a few phone numbers with what kind of sex act you'd get from calling them, a couple of swastikas, and a sentence written in large letters which screamed, "I've Been Framed!" I wanted to underline that one.

"Liam, what do want?" Marie didn't sound happy.

"I'm in jail."

"What'd you do?"

"Nothing. I didn't do a goddamned thing, but they think I beat..." My voice cracked. "They think I beat up Dawn. They think I tried to kill her."

All I could hear on the other end was laughter. Like everyone there had been listening in and thought I had delivered the funniest punch line they'd ever heard.

"Hello?" I yelled.

"This is a bad time, Liam. I can't leave now."

"I need your help. I didn't do it."

"Of course, you didn't," she said, her voice softening.

I could hear her breathing. I knew Marie must have been thinking about how to control the situation. She was concerned about how having her brother's arrest for attempted murder would affect Glenn's campaign.

"Let me see what I can do. Don't tell anyone about this."

Was she kidding?

"How is she, Liam?"

"The detective told me that she's in pretty bad shape. They think I did it, Marie. I would never—"

"I know. Listen, I'm going to have to make some calls. It might take a while. And I really can't do it now. People will start asking questions. They'd love something like this to bring down Glenn."

It warmed my heart that Marie had her priorities in order. I wanted to tell her that, but she had already hung up the phone.

"I'm all done," I told the guard.

"Just you wait," he replied. The bailiff seemed mesmerized by the centerfold. He got another eyeful of the picture, then slapped the magazine on his desk. He stood up without even attempting to hide the bulge in his pants.

He followed me to my cell. He was close behind me, breathing through his mouth, his breath licking my neck. I didn't think he'd try anything with me, but I had begun to realize that anyone I ran across was capable of doing most anything.

It was late and I sat alone in my cell. More prisoners had drifted in through the night. Why they put me alone in a cell while stuffing the other three cells with drunks, I didn't know. I recognized a few of them, and I could tell they knew me as well, but were avoiding eye contact. They sang, shouted out obscenities, and a few barfed-up whatever mix of drinks had caused them to get thrown into jail in the first place. An occasional scuffle would break out with one of the Hells Angels, which often ended quickly, accompanied by the crack of someone's head hitting the ground.

Hours passed with no sign of Marie, but I didn't expect she'd come through for me anytime soon. She had important people to entertain. I put my head down on what passed for a pillow. The mattress carried the faint scent of urine. Eventually, I fell asleep to the sounds of someone laughing uncontrollably down the hall.

I wasn't out long when I heard the bailiff shout.

"Okay, let's go."

Before my eyes could open, I heard the jingle of keys and the cell door opening.

I rose slowly. "Where?"

"Come on."

I followed the bailiff down the hall. A sheet of toilet paper hung from his pants. He led me back to the interrogation room where Detective Branch waited. His expression had changed, like he had been dreaming of something better in life, but knew that all he had to look forward to in this world was dealing with scum like me.

"We're letting you go. For now."

He eyed me like dog turd he couldn't get off of his shoe.

"You've got friends in high places. When the blood match comes in, though, I'm hauling your ass back in here. I'll make sure you fry for this."

"Why are you going after me? I don't get it."

"You mean other than the bloody shirt?"

"What made you come to my house last night?"

"Someone saw your truck in her driveway. They took down your license plate number."

"Someone saw me? Was it a man? Did he give you his name?"

Branch and Greene exchanged a look. I was right.

"You dragged me in because of an anonymous call?"

Branch reached into his coat pocket and pulled out a plastic bag. I couldn't see inside of it. He examined it for a moment before tossing it to me.

"We found this in your house."

There was a torn piece of paper inside the bag.

"Go on. Read it."

I straightened the bag out and studied the paper. I recognized Dawn's handwriting. "What is this?"

"Just read it."

It came from her diary. I knew she kept them. My hands trembled as I read her words. She said that she still loved me. That she believed in me. Without thinking, I held the bag to my chest, but Greene yanked it from my hand.

"Looks like she planned on leaving you," Greene said. "I'm betting that hurt. You tore out that page because it pointed to you. It incriminated you. You weren't going to let her go, were you?"

I leaned against the wall for support. "Someone is trying to set me up. I would never hurt Dawn. I love her. I don't know what's going on, but it has to do with my father's murder. I'm guessing Dane Lohan was involved."

"Watch what you say about him. He was a fine man." Branch lurched toward me like he was going to hit me.

I raised my hands. I was exhausted. I felt like an old man at the end of his life. "There's a guy out there. He's got the palest face you've ever seen. I don't know who he is, but he's behind this. He hurt Raven Andrews, and now he's hurt Dawn."

"She's dead," Branch said.

"What?"

"You heard me. She's dead. The doctor just called. How does it feel, Sol, to kill someone? Good? Indifferent? What? You ready to confess?"

I slid to the floor, my legs no longer able to support me. I couldn't breathe. I was choking on air. Branch grabbed me by the collar and pulled me up to my feet. He got so close to my face that I could see the fillings in his mouth.

"Come on. Get it off your chest. Tell me you did it. You'll feel better."

I shook my head and tried to turn away.

"Maybe we should take another look at your father's murder. We heard that the two of you had a big argument at the Beach Club. Then he turns up dead. Maybe you killed him. We never did check your alibi."

"Fuck you."

He threw a backhand to my face. It caught me flush on the cheek. I took a swing at him, but he grabbed my arm and threw me to the ground. I was too tired and ashamed to get up. I lay there, wanting so badly to cry, but not in front of him. I held it back. No matter what he did to me, I was not going to cry.

"Your lawyer's waiting. I'll get him."

He examined his hand as if ashamed of his reaction. I could taste the blood in my mouth, but I was numb to the pain.

The lawyer, Paul Michelson, greeted me like a close friend. I'd never seen him before, but he patted me on the back and told me a lot of stuff I wasn't ready to hear. He looked to be a little older than me, and I had to wonder if Marie had slept with him, too. The suit looked as if it had been hand-woven in Italy, and not a hair on his head was out of place. He looked sharp as hell. I had to give him that. Michelson kept telling me not to worry. He didn't seem to notice that I'd been smacked in the face. He did a lot of talking, but it sounded rehearsed, as if he were still in the process of learning to lie to his clients about their chances. He continued to drone on, but all I could think about was Dawn—and that I was the one responsible for her death.

He said he could drive me to my parents' house, but I told him to take me home. The sun had just started to rise when he dropped me off.

"I'll call you," he said.

He sounded just like I did right after I had my way with a girl.

CHAPTER THIRTY

The inside of my house looked as if a tornado had blown through it. My crap was spread all over the floor. Fucking bastards.

I went to the kitchen and saw that they had emptied out my cupboards as well. Cereal boxes and broken jars of jelly littered the floor. At least they hadn't taken my beer. I grabbed one and limped back to the leather chair in the living room, and then the phone rang.

"She was such a pretty girl. Too bad it had to happen. Maybe now you'll finally get it. You need to back off."

Then the line went dead. It was him. His phlegm-filled voice was cool and calm, like he was recommending which dish to order in a restaurant. The wind kicked up and blew open the front door, and the dust and the leaves came in from the outside and swirled around my feet. The air felt hot and dry, and the morning sun blasted my face. I pushed the door shut and slid to the floor, my back holding the door closed against the wind. I pictured Dawn fighting him off. She wouldn't have gone easily, not Dawn. I tried to imagine the terror that she must have felt, the confusion and the horror. Oh, Jesus. Not her. Not Dawn.

I'd killed her. Not the way the cops thought, but I had. If not for me, she'd be alive. If not for me...

And then I began to cry. I put my head to the floor and curled up like a little baby, and I cried myself to sleep.

The next two days were a mess. Marie, as I was learning, carried a lot of influence. Somehow she kept my arrest from being reported in the newspapers. But Dawn's murder was big news, and word had started to leak out that the police considered me a suspect. Hike and Lonnie were still surfing in Mexico, so word hadn't reached them. I had no idea when they'd return. I had no one to turn to. Detective Branch came out to question me further. The blood tests, he said, were back, and it was a match.

"Of course it was Dawn's blood. This guy is setting me up."

"You and your lawyer work that one out?"

"Are you even looking for the guy I told you about?"

"You know, the one thing I don't get," he said, ignoring my question, "is why you killed her? It must have been an accident, right? You just lost your temper. That's all. Things just got out of hand. I get it. You wouldn't be the first guy to lose it over a girl. We'll take that into consideration, you know."

"I didn't do it."

"We talked to the waitress who worked the night you and Miss Arnett were at Rosa's."

"She was drunk."

"Yeah? She told us that the two of you were arguing."

"We weren't arguing. We had a lot to sort out. I thought all you needed was a blood match. Why aren't you arresting me? Your case isn't working out is it?" I was acting tough, but I'm sure he saw through it. I felt like a little boy in a man's world.

"When we get all the evidence together—and make no mistake about it, we're damn close—our case will be so tight all the lawyers your family can buy won't be able to get you out of this. I'm sure your prison cell will be a great place to work on your tan."

He smiled at that, lit a cigarette, and walked to his car.

I wanted to attend Dawn's funeral, to say good-bye, but I knew I wouldn't be welcome. Not now. Not with the rumors flying about, but I couldn't stay in the house any longer. I had to do something. I had to do something for Dawn. I drove out to the desert. Dawn had a thing for native plants, and desert wildflowers were among her favorite. I longed for the open road and thought the drive to the desert would free my mind from the hell in La Bolsa. It didn't work out that way. Instead, the drive provided plenty of time for my mind to drift to the very things I was trying to hide from.

What was I doing with my life? I surfed, chased girls, and lived off of my family's money. Dawn may have been born to ride waves, but she was more than that. She was a teacher. She taught kids how to read and write. She taught them about how to be good and to do the right thing. I knew that sometimes her work got her down, but that only made her work harder to find a better way. She led a group of misfits trying to protect a goddamned marsh from being turned into a housing development. She went up against my father. Not many would do that. She put her heart into everything she did, knowing that she might fail, knowing that she might not be up to it. She didn't just create ripples, she created waves. Dawn mattered. The world had lost someone special when she died. What would have been lost if I had been the one killed and not Dawn? My family would be sad and so would a few friends, but I had to face it, the only ripple in life that I had caused was regret. Girls I led on—girls who thought I wanted more from them than a good night in bed. People who thought they could rely on me.

After Dawn and I had broken up, I could see now that I'd basically lived a lie. I lied to myself. And I bought the lie. *Just live the good life*, I said. Ride the waves, bed the girls, and have a good time. Feeling and caring just got in the way. There were better things to do than invest my time in something or someone other than myself. But now I realized that if I kept following that lie, I'd find myself alone. And maybe I was now. But still I wanted to keep living the lie because I needed to, because I found comfort and security in it. Maybe the day would come when I'd realize that the lies I had clung to were the only things that I had left, the only things that meant anything to me—and that scared the hell out of me.

I pulled off to the side of the road, just outside of Joshua Tree, and surveyed the landscape. I'd never seen much in the desert. Dawn had said it contained a hidden beauty that most didn't bother, or were unable, to see. I had tried, but I found it ugly and barren. Though I did have fond memories of the few nights we spent out here camping, lying on top of our sleeping bags, naked, and staring up at the desert sky.

Late fall may not be the best time for flowers, but with the help of a Girl Scout troop on a field trip, I found some desert marigold and Indian paintbrush that were still in bloom.

"They're so pretty, aren't they? I think I like them better than regular flowers," said one of the scouts, a young girl with dark red hair and bright blue eyes. Her scout uniform was a little big for her, but she didn't seem to mind. "You're picking these for a girl, aren't you?"

"I am, and a real special one, too. Thanks for helping me."

"We're Girl Scouts. It's what we do."

I wondered for a moment what the world would do to this girl when she grew up. I hoped she would be able to make her own world, and that no one like me would be there to fuck it up for her.

She admired the wildflowers she helped me pick and smiled. "Your girlfriend is going to love those."

"I hope she does. I really hope she does."

And Dawn would have loved them. I felt my eyes well up. I gave the girl a smile and walked back to my truck. I set the flowers down next to me on the seat, studying them for a moment. I decided that I agreed with the little girl. I liked them better than regular flowers, too.

CHAPTER THIRTY-ONE

I ROSE EARLY THE next morning, just after first light, and walked to the beach in my swim trunks, wildflowers in my hand. I couldn't bear to go to her gravesite, picturing her lying in a coffin, smothered beneath six feet of cold dirt. I looked out to the pier and stopped in my tracks. It was the paddle out. Surfers gathered in the ocean to pay their final respects to Dawn. She'd been a beautiful surfer, one of the few women the guys let ride with them. They never got the best of her, and they respected her for that.

A large circle of surfers huddled together just past the break. They held hands, their heads bowed in prayer. Bunches of flowers and leis floated in the center of the circle. The pier filled up with mourners, and a few dropped leis and wreaths into the ocean, near the circle of surfers. I crossed PCH and kept to the north side of the pier, determined not to be seen. *Only the good memories*, I tried to tell myself. *Only the good ones.*

I walked up to the water's edge and studied the surf. The Santa Anas and a nice southeastern swell had converged to create great waves. I glanced south and noticed the smoke continuing to build from the fire in the hills. We've had fires before, but I could see that this one was closing in on La Bolsa fast. I waded into the water, holding the flowers above my head, and then, when it got deeper, I swam, never letting the flowers get wet. I hadn't been in the ocean in a while, and the water felt cold, salty, and reassuring. I swam out past the break, where I said my own prayer. I prayed for Dawn's salvation, for her family, and though it shamed me, for myself as well.

I laid the flowers on the water. This would have made her happy, seeing her favorite desert flowers floating peacefully in the cool waters of the Pacific Ocean, each one following their own current, just like Dawn.

CHAPTER THIRTY-TWO

I HADN'T BEEN TO my parents' house since my arrest. Marie called a few times telling me to hang in there and that everything was going to be fine. My lawyer hadn't checked in with me, and when I called his office, his secretary assured me that he was on the case and that everything was going to be fine. Fine was the word of the day, but I didn't feel fine. The blood tests proved that it was Dawn's blood on my shirt. I didn't know what Branch was waiting for. He had seemed so eager to throw me back in jail. Maybe my lawyer was doing something after all.

The phone rang. I was hesitant to answer it as the rumor mill had sprung into action. I had already received a few calls from kind strangers accusing me of being a cold-blooded killer who deserved to burn in hell for eternity. But maybe this was Paul Michelson finally returning my call.

"I know you killed her, you piece of shit. I know you—"

I hung up. If that was Michelson on the phone, then I needed to find a new lawyer. I received about four calls like this a day. I didn't go out of the house much anymore. I couldn't handle the looks people gave me, followed by whispers, some more hushed than others: *That's him. That's the guy. You never can tell, can you? His poor mother.* They moved out of my way, frightened that I might just attack them, too. I just stayed at home, waiting for the police to come and arrest me.

I sat on my front porch, reading *On Her Majesty's Secret Service.* My sisters often teased me about my love of the Ian Fleming books, but I couldn't help it, I liked them. And right now, I needed James Bond in my life.

I heard a car pull up and saw Isabelle in her blue 1964 Chevy Impala. Isabelle was aware of the social graces, and until now, she had never made a surprise visit. She always phoned first to arrange an appropriate time to drop by. She wore a blue skirt and a white blouse, not a wrinkle to be seen. With her sunglasses on, she looked like a movie star. We had spoken a few times since my arrest, but this was the first we had seen each other since our last encounter at my parents' house.

Isabelle gave me a hug when I met her in the driveway. She brushed the hair out of my eyes, then held my hands.

"Liam," she said with a smile. "Are you holding up okay? I'm worried about you."

"Yeah. I'm okay, considering."

"Can I buy you a drink?" she asked.

"I'm not sure how well-stocked the bar is; but come on in, and let's see what I've got."

The radio was on KHJ, and a winded Bobby Tripp introduced the Strawberry Alarm Clock's "Incense and Peppermints."

"I like this song," she said.

My refrigerator was pretty empty. All I had was beer, Double Cola, and bologna. As if she read my mind, Isabelle called out that beer would be fine.

"That's good, because I drank all the French wine this morning."

I poured Isabelle's beer into a tall glass. I preferred to drink from the bottle. Isabelle sat on the couch, her legs comfortably folded under her, her white purse by her side.

"Thank you, but I could have handled the bottle," she said when I handed her the glass.

She took a long, slow sip of her beer. "Nice," she said.

She eyed my coffee table, looking for a safe place to rest her glass.

"I don't have coasters, so just put it on one of the magazines." I had a pile of surf magazines and other stuff on the table.

"Are you sure?" She smiled, staring at the latest issue of *Playboy.*

"I don't think Miss November will mind."

"Her dress is so pretty. But I guess that's not what interests you, is it?" She placed the glass directly on the cover girl's butt, and glanced at me, her eyebrows raised.

"That's going to ruin her dress," I said.

Isabelle smiled and scanned my living room. She pointed to a couple of abalone shells on the windowsill.

"They're so pretty."

Dawn and I had gone up to Point Conception for a weekend to camp and to dive for abalone. I wasn't great with a knife, but I'd managed to clean out the guts and keep the meat in fairly decent shape for grilling. I never claimed to be a great chef, but I went at the project with gusto, convincing myself that this was going to be my signature dish. I placed the grilled meat in warm corn tortillas with tomatillo salsa, but after the first bite, I knew that I had failed. Dawn pretended to enjoy them, politely dousing them in salsa. She was never a very good actress, but that didn't prevent her from trying. The next morning we cleaned out the shells in the ocean water and brought them home with us.

"I forgot all about that weekend," I said, after telling Isabelle the story. "God, she was so great. I can't believe she's gone." I studied the picture of the two of us that sat on the bookcase.

"Liam," Isabelle bit her lip, her eyes finding mine. "I know you didn't do it. You don't have it in you. Besides, anyone could tell how you felt about Dawn—and how she felt about you, for that matter."

"I can't believe what's happening. I always thought she'd be there. I always thought she'd be in my life."

"I liked her. We all did."

I felt myself nodding my head. "Ruby Tuesday" played on the radio, sounding like a Greek chorus.

"Liam, I know this isn't the time for this, but I need to explain something to you. Glenn and I don't have a, what's the word?... A traditional relationship. At least not like most people. There are things I can't give him. I want to. I want to be a good wife." Her eyes turned wet. "I know what you saw: Glenn and Marie. He's not bad, Liam. He's a good man."

"Isabelle—"

"He loves me. He does. He's a good man."

"He doesn't act like a good man, Isabelle. A good man wouldn't do that to his wife."

"I want you to understand, Liam. I love him. I do. But I can't give him the things a wife should be able to give her husband."

"Isabelle, what's—"

"I don't... I want to get better. I'm seeing a psychiatrist. I'm not crazy, Liam. It's not that. I just can't. He's been very patient, Glenn has, but he's a normal man."

"But how could Marie—"

Isabelle shrugged. "Marie is Marie. She's not like us, Liam. She never was."

She picked up her beer and held it with both hands. I got up and sat next to her on the couch. I took the glass from her and put it on the table, away from Miss November. I saw Isabelle's expression.

"The magazines are worth more than the table," I said.

She forced a smile. "Well, I just don't want you to hate Glenn. I know what's going on, and I accept it."

I held her hand. It felt cold and lifeless.

"He hurt me, Liam."

"What did Glenn do?"

"Not Glenn, Liam. Our father."

I felt my stomach drop.

"What are you talking about? Dad?"

She gazed out the window, staring at the sky as if it were a giant movie screen. It didn't appear that she liked what she saw. Flinching, she turned her face to mine and shut her eyes.

"It was my thirteenth birthday. I had finally become a teenager. I felt so proud, so grown up. Daddy had come to my room. He smelled of whiskey. He came to kiss me goodnight. He hugged me, and he kissed me behind the ear. Then he touched me. He whispered to me, telling me how pretty I had become and that he had to protect me from dirty boys. And he..."

I felt her whole body shudder. Maybe it was my body—I couldn't tell.

"He never touched Marie." She shrugged. "It was me he wanted. I don't know why. I don't know what I did to make him want to do that to me. I tried to make him not like me. I tried. But he would come in my room and tell me how much he loved me, how special I was, and I couldn't stop him."

I felt the bile rise from my gut. "Does Mom know?"

"No. She must never know." She glared at me, her voice fierce. "She must never know. It would kill her."

"Why are you telling me now?"

"I'm glad he's dead. I know you loved him, but I'm glad he's dead. We should all be glad that he's dead."

Tears streamed down her face, and she buried her head in my

shoulder, her body heaving. I held her close. She felt as cold as anything I had ever touched.

Who was my father? The man who taught me right from wrong? The man who disciplined me when I got caught cheating on a test in grade school? The man who returned extra change to a cashier? The man who worried about my future? The man who tried to get me back together with my old girlfriend? The man who everyone seemed to fear? The man who repeatedly raped his own daughter? I felt sick. Just how well did I know my father?

You grow up knowing that your parents have lied to you. Little white lies are what my mother called them: lies for your own good. What happens when the lies aren't white? What happens when you learn the truth? What happens when the man who you respected most in this world turns out to be bad, even evil? How, after knowing so much, can you find that you still love him?

He had killed Isabelle. In his own way, he'd killed her. He stole her soul from her, and I didn't know if Isabelle would ever be able to get it back. I held her until the sun started to fall into the horizon, leaving a bloodstained sky in its wake. Suddenly, she jerked and pulled away from me, her eyes dry now, but she looked older, much older than this morning.

"I'm sorry," she said. "I shouldn't have told you." She stood up and straightened out her skirt. I could see the mask forming again—the face she showed the world.

"Glenn has another reception tonight. The governor will be there."

"I don't care about Glenn. It's you I care about."

She put on her sunglasses, oblivious to the darkness falling outside.

"I'm fine."

"I love you, Isabelle. What you told me doesn't change anything."

"It will," she said. "It changed how Marie felt about me." Isabelle bit her lip. "You should go, Liam, far from here. You don't need any of this. You need to stay away from us. We're not good for you." She kissed my cheek and walked out the front door.

As I watched the taillights of her car fade in the distance, I couldn't help but wonder if she had killed my father. Not that I would blame her. The pale-faced guy, though, where did he fit in? Isabelle couldn't be part of this. Whoever was, also killed Dawn and maybe Dane Lohan and Eddie Capuano.

I grabbed another beer and went out onto the front porch. The La Bolsa pier was lit up for some kind of city event. I heard the rumble of motorcycles on Pacific Coast Highway and felt a chill come over me. Feeling exposed, I went back inside. Even though I knew he could get into my house anytime he wanted, I locked all the doors and windows and proceeded to drink myself into a restless sleep.

CHAPTER THIRTY-THREE

I WAS GETTING USED to waking up with a hangover. I downed a few aspirins with my coffee and took a long shower. I shaved and put on some nice slacks and a light blue button-down Oxford shirt. I caught my reflection in the mirror and had to admit that I still looked like shit. I drove out to the cemetery. From the amount of smoke that had filled the sky I could see the fire was spreading fast. I could taste the smoke and ash with every breath. I doubted I had the strength to visit her grave. I stood off in the distance, behind some bushes, and contemplated it from far away. The dirt was still fresh. I pictured her parents, broken and crying. Dawn was their only child, and now they were left with nothing. She had been their life and their future.

I thought about what my father had seen in me, how I might have been tied to his future. Had he truly been proud of me? After what Isabelle had revealed, did I even care? I knew why Dawn's parents were proud of her. Like me, they were forced to live without her now. I'd had her once. We were a couple, and she saw her future with me. And then I let her go, and then I got her killed.

I gathered the nerve to walk down to her grave. I was done crying. I felt so numb now, I didn't know if I could produce another tear. I sat in the grass, next to her grave, and talked to her. Her grave marker hadn't been placed yet. I knew she wasn't there, not really. I was talking to the wind. I tried to pretend she could hear me, but even if she could, I questioned whether she'd be interested in anything I had to say.

Afterward, I walked to my father's grave. "Loving Father and Husband," the marker said. I tried to find some kind of emotion, but I was on empty. I couldn't hate him. I wanted to. I knew it would be easier if I could.

I saw the spot where the Kiyans had stood after his funeral. They were part of this. I didn't know how or why—maybe they didn't know either—but they were in this.

I drove down PCH and parked across the highway from the Kiyans' first fruit stand in La Bolsa. The Kiyans, I guessed out of pride or because this is where it all began, occasionally worked at this stand. I sat in my truck and waited. Maybe Mrs. Kiyan would come by today, and I could talk to her. I didn't want to go to her house—not with the cousins there.

The winds had died down, and the sky turned a charcoal gray. You couldn't tell where the fire was, but you knew it was near, and that it was racing toward La Bolsa like an animal running down its prey. The hillsides that were so close were now only a faint outline, as if someone had taken a giant eraser to them. Watching the cars driving by on PCH, I could see the concern on the drivers' faces. The fear that the winds would whip up again during the night and push the fires even closer, perhaps overtaking us while we slept, was on everyone's mind.

I got tired of turning the radio dial, so I kept it on Boss Radio. I went through Robert W. Morgan all the way to The Real Don Steele, from the Blues Magoos to the Young Rascals. Four hours and no one showed up to open the fruit stand. Maybe it wasn't a good day to sell strawberries. I got out of my truck and waited for a break in the traffic. I didn't think the fruit stand was going to reveal anything, but since I was here, I thought I'd look around.

The scent of strawberries overpowered the tiny space. It was like being trapped in an elevator with someone who showered with stale perfume. On the wall someone had scrawled "Go home Japs." It appeared that someone had tried to wash it off, but the message refused to be erased. I don't know why they didn't just paint it over. I didn't see anything of interest. As I walked out, something on the ground near the entrance caught my eye. I knew what it was, but I bent down anyway. Black cigarettes, smoked halfway down, lying in a neat little pile. He'd been here, too. Was he working for the Kiyans, or was he terrorizing them?

I went back to my truck and watched the cars speed by on PCH. I had no idea what to do next, but I couldn't go back to jail for killing Dawn while her real killer was out there. I was out of my league. I needed to be like Marshal Dillon, but I felt a hell of a lot like Barney Fife.

I heard a loud blast of engines roaring up Pacific Coast Highway. Satan's Council was a motorcycle gang out of La Bolsa. They acted like every other biker gang you'd see stalking PCH, but these guys surfed as well. When they weren't out doing damage on the road or puking their guts out in the parking lot of a roadside bar, they'd be on their boards in the water. You'd think the cosmic grace of the endless waves and the timelessness of the ocean would have softened them, but they enjoyed drawing blood and blades as much as the Hells Angels. Yet they made peace with most of the locals. Bobby Dix rode with them a lot, and he wouldn't tolerate anyone pissing on his beach.

I saw Dix on his black 1965 Harley Davidson Pan Head, riding just to the outside of the pack. As I watched them ride by, I thought that Bobby Dix might just have some answers for me. I'd seen him that night at the bar at Rosa's with the pale-faced guy. They didn't seem to be friends, but maybe Dix knew some things about him that I should know.

I turned on the wipers to clear the ashes from my windshield, and followed the Council up PCH to a biker bar on the outskirts of Sunset Beach. The Hog's Tale looked like an accident waiting for an ambulance. It was a part-damaged boxcar built into an old auto repair garage. I parked on the street so as not to tangle with any of the bikes in the parking lot, their motorcycles more sacred to them than their mothers. One scrape could mean a fight that you'd never be able to talk your way out of. I watched them as they strutted into the bar, on guard and in uniform: bandanas, leather jackets, worn Levi's, and steel-tipped boots. I waited a few minutes before following them inside. With my blue Oxford, pressed khakis, and Keds with no socks, I was going to fit in just fine here.

I opened the door and was greeted with a blast of cigarette smoke. The Sonics' "Psycho" blasted out of the jukebox. The Hog's Tale reeked of body odor, dope, cigarettes, and just a touch of vomit. I didn't see many girls, just a dozen or so bikers sitting around talking and drinking. Unlike in the movies, the place didn't go silent when I entered, but I could feel everyone's eyes on me and the tension level rising. I put my hands in my pockets and tried to appear calm.

A voice shot out, "Who ordered the turd?"

I ignored the question and headed to the bar and sat on a stool, hoping that Bobby Dix would see me. I didn't want to troll the place looking for him.

"Liam Sol. What the fuck are you doing here?" Bobby Dix said as he emerged from the bathroom. He patted me on the shoulder like we were old friends. I felt the tension in the bar drop. I guessed having the Bobby Dix seal of approval was all I needed. "You want a beer?"

I shook my head. "Can we talk outside?"

"Two Buds," he told the bartender. "If you don't drink, they're going to think you're a narc. I don't need that."

We sat at a battered picnic bench in front of The Hog's Tale and watched the traffic flow down PCH.

"So, I hear that the cops have you pegged for killing Dawn. I know you didn't do it. You ain't no killer. No, sir, you don't got that in you." He took a big drink from his bottle. "I always liked her. She was all right."

"Everybody liked Dawn."

"Somebody didn't," he said.

I stared at my bottle of beer.

"After my father died, I saw you at the bar at Rosa's. You were sitting next to this guy with a real pale face, jet-black hair. You remember him?"

Bobby Dix shook his head. "Don't sound familiar."

"Looked like the two of you were talking."

"I said, it don't sound familiar."

A diesel truck sputtered down PCH. The driver appeared unsure of himself, as if the steering wheel was too big for him to handle. The guy had no business driving that rig. I hoped he'd realize it and pull off to the side of the road, but I doubted it. I was sure the driver believed he was in complete control of everything.

"That guy, Bobby, the one at Rosa's. He's the guy who killed my father. He's the guy who murdered Dawn. He killed Eddie Capuano, and I'm betting he killed Dane Lohan. I think he wants me dead, too."

I took a big hit of the beer, but I found that it no longer held any taste.

"Do you know who he is?" I asked.

"Your old man, he did all right by me." Bobby Dix tapped the side of his beer bottle. "You know why no one ever gave you no trouble? Your dad would have had them killed. That's the truth. I ain't lying. He told me that flat out."

I tried to take that in, but pushed it aside. He was dodging my question. "Who is he, Bobby?"

Bobby Dix closed his eyes as if he were trying to push the pale-faced guy's image from his brain. "This guy you're talking about. I don't know him, okay? But if I did, I'd listen to him. I'd listen to him real good. I seen a lot of shit, Liam. I done a lot, too. This guy, he don't sound like he's all together. He sounds like his blood got mixed up with a fuckin' ghoul of some kind. Do what he says, man. Just do what he says."

Bobby Dix stood up and headed for the front door of the bar.

"What if I don't?"

He stopped, but didn't look back at me.

"Your dad ain't here to protect you no more. I think all you can do is to get on your knees and pray, and hope to heaven that God likes you enough to save your ass."

He walked inside the bar. A quick rush of cigarette smoke and rock music blew out, and then, as soon as the door shut, the quiet returned. I finished off my beer. It had turned warm and stale. I glanced at the table and saw something carved into the wood. I cleared some of the dust away. It read, "God is dead." Great, even praying wasn't going to help me now.

CHAPTER THIRTY-FOUR

"You know how to use one of these?"

"Yes," I lied. I'd shot at rabbits and deer in the hills with my father, but that was with a 22 caliber rifle. Still, I was pretty sure I could figure out a pistol. The bigger question was whether I'd be able to use it when the moment arrived.

The salesman must have been about fifty, with a crooked toupee and a handlebar moustache. His voice sounded hoarse, and he was breathing hard, as if one of his lungs was working against him.

"It's a Colt Cobra .38 Special. Jack Ruby used one of these to kill Oswald."

"It looks small."

"It is. Just a two-inch barrel. But believe me, it's loud and it packs a punch."

"How much?"

He told me, and I took out my wallet.

"There's a waiting period."

"What do you mean?"

"I mean you can't take it home now. There's a five-day waiting period."

He saw the frustration in my eyes. He looked around to make sure that no one would be able to hear his next words.

"I'm sure we can arrange something," he said, looking at my wallet. "Uncle Sam don't need to know everything."

"Is this legal?" I asked.

"You want the gun now or not?"

I told him I did.

"Just add fifty bucks to the price."

"Seriously?"

"You can always fill out the form and wait the five days."

"I'll buy the gun now."

"Don't tell anyone where you bought this. I'm serious," he whispered.

"I won't, don't worry. I'm going to need bullets, too." He gave me a look as if he were reconsidering our deal. I put my hands in my pockets to keep them from shaking. He nodded and then wheezed his way back to the stockroom.

As I walked out of the store I could feel his eyes on me, probably wondering what the hell I was planning on doing with the same kind of pistol that killed Lee Harvey Oswald.

I loaded the gun in my truck. My hands felt unsteady. I was breathing hard as if I'd just run a marathon. I tried to imagine pulling the trigger, but the only image that came was of me standing frozen while the pale-faced guy beat Dawn to death with a baseball bat.

I drove out to the Kiyans' place. The pistol sat next to me, holding me hostage. I planned to keep the gun in the car. I didn't want any trouble. If the cousins were there, I'd drive away and figure out another way to talk to Mrs. Kiyan. I just didn't know when or where the pale-faced guy would turn up next.

Driving up to their farm was like riding through a ghost town. No one was in the field, no cars were parked in the driveway, and their screen door banged against the doorframe as the wind began to pick up again. I sat in the truck, turned off the radio, rolled my window down, and listened. All I could hear was the wind, the screen door slamming, and the occasional car driving by.

Something didn't feel right. The hairs on the back of my neck rose, and I stifled the urge to flee. I grabbed my gun. It was small and light, but it felt heavy in my hand. I scanned the area, looking for any sign of life as I walked up to the front door, which was wide open. I held the screen to keep it from banging against the frame, and paused before stepping inside. The interior of the house was immaculate. Everything appeared normal until I got to the kitchen. The refrigerator door was ajar, and two bowls of noodles and a bowl of strawberries sat on the kitchen table, both barely touched. A half glass of milk and a full cup of tea sat next to them. The chairs had been pulled back from the table, and a waste can stood next to one of the chairs, a foul odor drifting out from it.

"Don't move."

I dropped the gun. Instinctively, I went to pick it up.

"Don't do it." I recognized the voice. It came from one of the cousins who beat me up the last time I visited.

I raised my hands and turned to the voice. It was the smaller of the two. He held what I assumed to be a samurai sword, and he pointed it directly at my throat.

"What you want?" His hands shook.

"I came to talk to Mrs. Kiyan. It's important. What's going on?"

He lowered the sword, tears forming in his eyes.

"Joy got sick. She start shaking. Can't stop. Can't breathe. Her mother can't wait for ambulance. Take her to hospital herself."

"Have you heard anything from them?"

He shook his head. "Someone call this morning and ask how the strawberries tasted for breakfast. My bro's outside. He's looking for him. Bad guy out there."

He cast his eyes down, as if he felt shame for not being able to protect the family.

"This guy, he's like a ghost. He's gotten into my home, too. He's killed people. He likes it." Through the kitchen window I saw a flock of birds flying directly into the smoke from the fire. "You need to call the police."

He raised the sword. "I will kill him. When I see him, I kill him."

Good luck with that, I thought. I picked my gun off the floor and walked out, leaving him alone in the kitchen with his sword shaking in his hands, ready to attack an enemy he would never see coming until it was too late.

I stopped off at a Richfield gas station to use the bathroom. I washed my face and caught my reflection in the mirror. My eyes were bloodshot, and I saw something in my face I'd never seen before: pure fear. I thought about how it would feel to die at the hands of a stranger—never knowing why he picked you out of the herd. The gun wasn't going to be much help if I continued dropping it at every strange sound that came my way. Someone wanted the Kiyans' land. Offers were one thing, but now they'd tried to kill a child. I could only think of one person who was capable of this, and I cursed myself for never putting it together sooner. Archibald Roth. Wanting the land, I could understand. That's how he made his living. But why he'd want my father killed was something I couldn't fathom. They were partners. Roth probably had more money than anyone I knew, including my father. But I knew there were people in this world for whom there would never be enough money and, I was sure, never be enough power. Roth had once told my dad that the coastline was their kingdom. Perhaps in Roth's mind, two kings were one too many.

CHAPTER THIRTY-FIVE

I NEVER LIKED BEING too far from the ocean. Once the scent of salt left my senses, I always got the feeling I was in a foreign territory. Temperature-wise, West Covina was as different from La Bolsa as hell was from heaven. The valleys were always about thirty degrees hotter than the coast. And even though the mountains were only a couple of miles away, I knew on most days they couldn't be seen because of the smog that sat heavily on the valley floor. Today, though, the winds had blown out the dirty air. Mount Wilson and Mount Baldy appeared so close I thought I could hit them with a toss of a rock. The San Jose Hills to the southeast looked like they made for great hiking, but the bulldozers were there, too, carving craters into the earth. This land had once grown rows of citrus and walnut trees. Now, a mad dash was on to rip them out and see who could build the ugliest housing tracts. It wasn't much different than what my father had done. It just looked worse here. Some kids rode by on their Stingray bicycles, glaring at us. I could see they weren't happy about someone tearing up this field either. I'm sure it had been a great place for them to play. Even though it was burning up outside, I put on a jacket to hide my gun.

I stood on one of the last bits of open land left in the city. A weathered, clapboard farmhouse stood abandoned and alone, waiting to be replaced by a number of stucco boxes. Men hammered stakes into the ground, and tractors coughed brown smoke into the air. Archibald Roth stood tall in a white cowboy hat, long-sleeved black shirt, pressed jeans, and dark snakeskin boots. He was a man who dressed like the Old West, yet he was also a man compelled to pave over any trace of it from the earth. All he was missing were six-shooters packed into twin holsters. He studied me, his eyes squinting from the high sun.

"What would I want with a strawberry field?" he asked.

I glanced at one of the bulldozers as it flattened an old oak tree into the ground. "You tell me. My dad didn't want to buy it. Bonnie Kiyan told me that much."

"She's a looker, ain't she? If you haven't done it yet, you got to make a point of getting some of that Oriental pussy sometime." He smirked at me. "But you've probably been there a few times yourself. Haven't you, partner?"

He knelt down and picked up a handful of the brown earth, almost fondling it. "Yes, sir, they sure do like getting it from white men." He grinned at me. "I guess they liked Mexicans, too."

Roth bit his lip and then let the loose soil slip through his fingers.

"It's just dirt to most folks. But I can change this dirt into gold. No, I knew your daddy didn't want to buy up the Kiyan land, so I didn't push him too hard. He wasn't going to budge. But, yeah, after he died I made some inquires. Kiyans don't want to sell. I can wait. In the meantime, there's more land out there. There's always more land."

He rose and wiped the leftover dirt from his hands.

"You didn't send anyone to talk to them? Or to me?" I swallowed hard. "To Dawn Arnett's?"

"I heard about your girlfriend. They think you did that though, don't they?"

"I didn't do it."

"Neither did I," he said, and then he gave me a wink.

I was tempted to take a swing at him, but held back.

"I saw you talking to her boyfriend at the DMZ. What was that about?"

"Yeah, that's right. I talked to him. Not a very impressive man. She could have done a hell of a lot better." He gave me the once-over. "But maybe even he was a step or two above you."

I let what he said pass, but it struck a nerve. "What were you two talking about?"

"He needed a little money, and I needed his little hippie group to call off their protests over some land we wanted for the Beach Club. He made the right deal. Your daddy didn't live to see it, but we're finally going to be able to build that marina he always wanted. People like that hippie talk a good game, all peace and love and save the planet, but nothing cuts to the truth of a man like cold hard cash."

A lone seagull circled overhead. It was as out of place as I was.

Archibald Roth marched over to the farmhouse, unbuckled his pants, and started to relieve himself. "I think you oughta go back home and take care of your momma. I hear she's been hitting the bottle pretty hard lately. You ever wonder why your daddy didn't buy the Kiyans' land?"

"What are you saying?"

"I'm just asking questions. You ever wonder why the Kiyans keep Joy hidden away from the world. You ever get a good look at that girl?"

"Someone tried to kill her. Who would do that?"

Archibald Roth let out a little chuckle and peered over his shoulder at me.

"Now that Marie's in charge, everything's changed. You should have taken over, son. Everything would have been different. You had your chance."

He finished his business and turned my way, his pants still undone, exposing himself to me. "Anything else you'd like to know?" he asked. Roth zipped his pants and walked up to me. He patted my jacket, letting me know he knew I had a gun there.

My hands turned clammy. "I'll find out what you have to do with all this," I said, my voice cracking like a little boy's.

"Mr. Roth, when do you want them to bulldoze the house?"

It was my cousin, Carlos. If he was shocked to see me, he didn't show it. He didn't say anything, but he glared at me like I was something that needed to be taken out with the garbage.

"Carlos works for me now, Liam. I find that he's a good man to have around. Doesn't mind getting his hands dirty, if you know what I mean."

Then he whispered in my ear, his breath hot and sticky. "Go back to the beach, surfer boy." And then he put his lips together and made a kissing sound.

A bad taste filled my mouth, one that I didn't think I'd ever be able to completely wash out. He made me sick. Whether he had anything to do with my father's death or not, I wanted to shoot him. I wanted to shove the barrel of my gun down his throat and watch him gag and sweat and beg for his life, and then I wanted my face, Felix Sol's son, the brother of Marie and Isabelle, to be the last thing he ever saw. But all I managed to do was to schlep back to my truck, my head down, scared out of my wits, doubting that if the opportunity ever came, I'd have the guts to pull the trigger.

As I grabbed the door handle of my truck, the blast of a gunshot ripped through the air. I turned back and saw the lone seagull fall dead from the sky.

Archibald Roth stood by his pickup, a smoking rifle resting in his hands. His eyes were set firmly on mine, and then he smiled. A sudden, hot gust of wind came up, blowing dust and dirt that encircled Roth and hid him from view, as if the devil were calling him down for a friendly visit.

CHAPTER THIRTY-SIX

I'D BEEN IN the emergency room at La Bolsa Community Hospital more times than I could remember. My visits consisted of some kind of bodily injury: broken arms, dislocated shoulders, and my first and only concussion. Each of these injuries had been accompanied by a two-hour wait in the emergency room.

The ER was strangely quiet, as if it were resting for the coming night. There were two families with their kids in the waiting room. One was holding a bloody nose; the other nursed a bump on his head with a bag of ice. It was still too early for the drunks and the bar fight crowd. Once the sun went down, it would be a much different and uglier scene.

The nurse behind the counter looked bored and seemed disappointed when she saw no visible wounds or blood streaming from my body. She handed me a clipboard and a pencil.

"Take a seat and fill this out." She gave me another look. "What's wrong with you, anyway?"

"Nothing." I handed back the stuff she gave me. "I'm trying to find a patient: Joy Kiyan. She must have come in a few hours ago. She may have already been admitted."

She frowned. "I just got on the clock." She picked up another clipboard and scanned the list of names. She turned to the next page and bit her lip.

"Are you a relative?"

"Is she okay?"

"I'm sorry. I can't give you any information, I—"

"She'll be fine."

I turned to the familiar voice. Bonnie Kiyan stood in the doorway, holding a cigarette and a cup of coffee in the same hand. Her other hand combed through her long dark hair. She wore Levi's and a black Jefferson Airplane T-shirt.

"Why are you here? How'd you hear about this?"

"I went to your house."

I motioned her to follow me outside onto an empty courtyard.

"I think the guy who poisoned Joy was the same guy who killed Dawn and my father."

"Why do you think Joy was poisoned?"

"One of your cousins told me."

"Don't believe either of them. Those two are fresh off the boat. They probably think we're still in World War II."

Bonnie tossed her cup in the trash and took a long drag off her cigarette. I caught the scent and felt the hairs on my arm rise. Cloves. It had to be a coincidence.

"Something got her sick. It could have been the damn pesticides. I've been trying to get them off the DDT. That's bad stuff."

"It wasn't DDT. Someone is sending your family a message to sell the land."

"No one's come by lately." She took another drag, but this time I saw that her hand shook.

"I need a drink," she said.

We went to a bar just down the street, hidden between a hardware store and a sandwich shop. Only a few people were inside, but we were the youngest by about thirty years. We found a table in the back. An Andy Williams song played on the jukebox, the same one I'd heard when I first visited Mrs. Kiyan.

"What's going on?" I asked.

Bonnie took a sip of her beer. "I can't get my mom to sell the land. If it gets rezoned and we get forced out, we won't make anywhere near the money that we're being offered now."

"Who wants to buy?"

"Your sister."

I stiffened. "Marie?"

Bonnie narrowed her eyes at me and then nodded.

"Not Archibald Roth?"

"Oh, he's asked, but it's your sister who's been pushing it."

I sat back in my chair. Nothing made sense. I felt as if I were looking at a compass that pointed north and south at the same time.

"You told me that evening on the pier that my dad didn't want to buy your land. And now my sister wants it?"

"Your dad was very good to our family. When my parents were interned during the war, my mother said he paid for the taxes and the upkeep of their land. When they got out, the farm had been kept in perfect condition. A lot of other Japanese families lost everything when they were relocated. If it weren't for your dad, I don't know what would have happened. My father wanted to repay him, but your dad refused. He said what the government did to our family was a sin."

This was all news to me. The compass was pointing east and west now as well.

"That's why you were at his funeral. But I don't understand. Why would he do that?"

Bonnie shrugged. I could tell that she was becoming uncomfortable. She pulled a pack of cigarettes from her purse. "It was never discussed. 'Mr. Sol is a very fine man' is all my mother would say."

Bonnie lit up another cigarette and inhaled deeply.

"What kind of cigarettes are those?"

"Black Clove. They're imported. Bought them at a head shop in Venice."

I thought about what Roth had said about Joy.

"Are you okay?" Bonnie asked.

"How old is Joy?"

"Why?"

"When did your father die?"

"What are you... go to hell." She threw her beer at me then stood up. "Fuck you, Sol. Fuck you. Stay away from Joy. She's a Kiyan. Stay away or I'll make sure you... she has nothing to do with your family. She's a Kiyan. You hear that? A Kiyan. You come near her, I'll..." She stormed out of the bar, leaving the sentence unfinished. I sat there, drenched in beer, taking in the lingering scent of the same brand of cigarette that the pale-faced man smoked.

I remembered the searing look Marie gave the Kiyans after my father's funeral. I was starting to get the answers to questions I'd never thought to ask. I didn't want to go back to my parents' house. It no longer felt like the home I grew up in. It was as if my family was about to wither away, becoming something I would no longer be able to recognize. Maybe my father was the one who had held us all together, or maybe the whole time it had all just been an illusion.

I ordered another beer, but sat at the bar this time. The TV was on, and the reporter spoke in a grim tone. The winds had suddenly increased their velocity, causing the fire to jump the firebreak. The inferno was blasting toward La Bolsa, faster than anyone had anticipated, and the firemen were not equipped to stop it. The La Bolsa police and fire department called a meeting to discuss possible evacuations.

"This is a bad one," the bartender said. "You can feel it. Look at that." He showed me his arm. "Hair's standing on end: goose bumps. I haven't felt like this since Normandy."

This wasn't new to us. Over the years more than a few fires had found their way close to our home, but we never had to evacuate. This time, though, everything told me it was going to be worse. As much as I wanted to walk away from my family, I couldn't do it. I left my beer on the bar and walked out to my truck. I needed to go to my parents' house. I had to see if they needed any help.

The Santa Anas rarely lasted this long. The thermometer at United California Bank read ninety-one degrees.

The road heading south was empty except for the occasional fire truck, its lights and sirens blaring. A long line of cars crawled by on the northbound lanes. The worried faces of the drivers and passengers told the story. They were no longer in control of their lives. Either the fire would take everything, or it wouldn't. Life or death was that simple. It was random and uncontrollable. We couldn't help but try to bring sense to the world, though we knew it was out of our hands. I didn't know what that said about us. I didn't know if that made us pathetic or noble.

As I stopped at the light on Pacific Coast Highway and Canyon Road, I couldn't help but notice the number of surfers in the water. The strong swell and the wind had shaped some insane waves. It was a surreal scene. The hillsides were on fire, the smoke blowing low over the ocean, and the boys on their boards were riding heartbreakingly beautiful waves as the world burned around them. The sun, peering through the smoke, looked like the tip of a dying cigarette.

CHAPTER THIRTY-SEVEN

THE PALE-FACED MAN

HE'D HAD ENOUGH of the surfer. Even after he killed the guy's girlfriend, the surfer kept asking questions. The surfer shouldn't have been able to walk the streets. He should still be behind bars.

He was proud of how he'd set him up for the girl's murder, but it hadn't worked out the way he wanted. Anyone who didn't have the juice of a rich family would have been locked up for good. He touched the side of his face. His cheek felt sore and tender from the hard elbow thrown by the surfer's ex-girlfriend. She'd turned out to be a fighter and hard to kill. The pale-faced man didn't like fighters. They were unpredictable and dangerous. He needed control, because once that was taken from him, anything could happen.

He'd thought he had the jump on her, but she had surprised him. She grabbed a baseball bat she must have hidden somewhere and took a hard swing at him. He caught the bat as it connected with his ribs. He pulled it from her and swung it at her head. The girl staggered, and he hit her again, knocking her to the ground. She rolled over on her stomach, and as he grabbed her from behind, she caught him with a hard elbow to the face. The girl crawled to the bat, blood pouring from the wound to her head. He could see she was losing consciousness from the loss of blood. He grabbed the bat and knelt down next to her, and then he whispered in her ear: "Liam sent me." But she never heard his words. She was already gone.

And now it was the surfer's turn. The dumb fuck kept putting his ass where it didn't belong. He wouldn't let up. He kept asking questions, kept nosing around. After seeing him at the strawberry farm and later with the Jap girl at the bar, the pale-faced man knew the time was now.

Most of the time, he killed because it was a job—a job that he was good at it. But the act also gave him pleasure. That, he could not deny. But to kill someone who deserved to die—someone who ignored your will—well, that was the ultimate experience. He was going to lead him to his execution. The pale-faced man was going to enjoy this.

CHAPTER THIRTY-EIGHT

I DROVE UP TO the house. Glenn stood in the doorway, watching the sky. I didn't want to deal with him, but there he was, in my way, as usual. I could tell he had seen me, but he didn't react.

"Let me by, Glenn."

"You're really fucking things up, Liam."

I didn't have time for this shit.

"Can you move, please?"

"You have no idea, do you?"

"What the hell are you talking about?"

He finally looked at me. His eyes as gray as the smoke that blanketed the sky.

"How many people have died because of you?"

"What do you know?" I grabbed him and pushed him hard up against the door.

"We can't protect you. Marie can't get you out of this. There's no one left for you to run to. You're on your own now, Liam. You're on your own."

"You don't know shit," I said. I pushed him aside and stormed into the house. Marie ran down the stairs and surprised me by giving me a hug.

"The police were here, Liam," she whispered urgently. "They're looking for you. They're going to arrest you. I'm sorry. They say they found more evidence. Liam, why?"

I pulled away and held her shoulders. "I didn't do it, Marie. I didn't do it."

She shook her head, her eyes pleading with me. "Liam. You need to go. You need to go now."

I took a step back. "What are you saying?"

I heard footsteps behind me. It was Glenn. "Just do what she says, Liam. You need to leave."

"Where's Mom?"

Marie shook her head. "The police will be back, Liam. You need to go, far away from here. Go to Mexico. Hang out there until I get this all fixed."

"Where's Mom?"

I started for the kitchen, but Marie stopped me. I could have pushed her aside, but it was becoming clear that my mother wanted nothing to do with me.

"Go now, before the police get here. Please, Liam. I'll fix this, I swear, but you need to leave."

I took a few steps back. I was being set up. I couldn't see a way out for me. Either I was going to die in jail like Eddie Capuano or get killed in La Bolsa. I decided to take my chances with the pale-faced guy. Maybe I'd get lucky.

I looked at Marie. Her head was down. She couldn't face me. I felt like I was held under a wave I couldn't swim out from.

"I didn't do it," I said. I walked outside. The smell of the burning brush from the hillsides spread over me like a deadly virus.

I knew I couldn't take my truck. If the cops were looking for me, they'd know what I was driving. I was going to have to switch cars. I felt as if I were in some twisted version of *The Fugitive*. Except my one-armed man was a cigarette-addicted psychopath. I parked my truck off the driveway and out of view of the house. As much as I wanted to lift Glenn's car, I knew it would be obvious I had taken it. I went into the garage where Isabelle kept her Impala. I grabbed her keys from the rack where we kept the extra sets.

Before driving off, I took a last look at the house. My mother watched me from her upstairs bedroom. I waved to her, and then she slowly pulled the drapes shut. I steered the Impala down the driveway, wondering how my mother could think that her only son was a murderer.

The only way to save myself was to get to the pale-faced guy: the one who killed my father and Dawn, the one who killed Eddie Capuano and maybe Dane Lohan. Whether Archibald Roth sent him or not, whether he was a lone killer or not, it didn't matter. I had to get to him. I didn't know if I could stop him, but I had no choice. I was done running.

I drove down PCH. The surfers had disappeared, as if the ocean had swallowed them in one giant gulp. The smoke from the fires now blocked out the sun entirely, leaving in its wake a world basked in permanent dusk. The water was an unnatural shade of gray, as if some vandal had poured poison into the ocean, leaving it to die a slow and lonely death.

I needed time to think. I parked away from the highway on a bluff that overlooked the sea. I wanted to surf. I wanted to take the power and force of the ocean and make it mine. I wanted to feel my heart race and know that the next wave might just be better than the last. All I wanted to do was ride the blue waves under an even bluer sky. I wanted to feel the wind rip through my hair, the taste of salt water fresh on my lips, and have a beautiful girl waiting for me on the sand, her arms open and welcoming. A cold beer next to an open fire as the sun kissed another day good-bye. I wanted the girl to look into my eyes and tell me I was the one. I was the only one. But this time I wouldn't run away. This time I wouldn't leave. This time I'd tell her that she was absolutely the one for me, and that she had always been the only one, and that I would forever be there for her. And then I'd take her hand, and we'd walk down to the water, the colors of the sunset bursting bright like a fireworks display. We'd see our future on the horizon. And we'd smile. Because we'd know, we'd know that we were all that mattered and that we'd never, ever be without the other.

"We could travel the world together," she had once said. "I love you. You're the one for me, Liam. I've always known it. You're the one." Good dreams can turn into nightmares in the blink of an eye.

I got out of the car and walked to the end of the bluff. I had always believed there would be time to make up for my mistakes. That everything would work out in the end. That those I loved would always be there. That they'd catch me when I'd fall, and somehow I'd be newer and better than ever. But the joke was on me. Because the only one who truly cared that I was alive was the very person who wanted me dead.

On the beach below, a sea lion was caught in a fisherman's net. It struggled, futilely, to free itself. That's when I heard the gunshot. I ducked behind the car for cover. I didn't know where the shot had come from. There were no cars on Pacific Coast Highway. Ashes fell around me like ghostly snowflakes.

The sea lion was no longer struggling. The bullet had put an end to that. Across the highway, I saw movement in the brush on the hillside. I rose up just a bit to get a better look, and then the windshield exploded. I hit the ground, curled up on a carpet of broken glass. The next shot blew off the side view mirror. He had me trapped, and I realized my gun was resting safely on the passenger seat of the car. The pale-faced man had found me. He must have followed me from my parents' house.

I knew if I was going to have any chance at all, I needed to get my gun. I crawled to the driver's side door, the body of the car shielding me. As soon as I opened the door, the bullets started flying. How many guns did he fucking have? I scrambled for my weapon, glass raining down on me. I fell back to the ground, struggling to keep a firm grip on the pistol as I held it in my trembling hand.

My shirt was soaked with sweat. All I could hear was the ringing in my ears and the pounding of my heart. And then I heard the sirens. I peered under the car and saw three police cars and an ambulance race north, away from the fire, up Pacific Coast Highway. I scrambled inside the Impala and started the car. I kept my head low while I hit the gas and followed the cop cars, waiting for the next shot.

I didn't raise my head until about a half mile later. I had no idea where the cops were headed, but I followed them as long as I could. They turned on Ocean, and I assumed they were headed to the hospital. I stayed on PCH and as I approached Main, I checked in my rear view mirror only to see that my own truck was barreling down on me. There was some distance between us, but he was closing the gap fast. A new wave of fear overtook me. He was at the house. He was following me. He was taunting me by taking my truck. His message clear: I had nowhere to hide.

I pulled a quick U-turn and headed down Main, driving past my truck. It was too dark to see the pale-faced man, but I caught the glow of his cigarette. I parked the car in front of a fire hydrant. As I ran out of the Impala, I looked back, but saw no signs of my truck. Even though the sun had just set, Main Street was empty. The fires had kept everyone close to home. I ran down Orange and ducked into the DMZ. Behind the bar, Dex's eyes widened when he saw me with the gun in my hand.

"The cops are looking for you, Liam."

"I know. I didn't do what they said I did. You have to believe me. There's a guy after me. Pale guy, jet-black hair, smoker. He's the guy. He's setting me up."

Dex pulled a shotgun from behind the bar. "What do you need?"

"I need a telephone, and then you never saw me."

He nodded and pointed toward his office. I ran inside, grabbed the phone, and dialed the operator.

"La Bolsa Police Department. It's an emergency."

"One moment, please," she responded.

A framed picture on Dex's desk caught my eye. He was in uniform, smiling, proud, a pretty girl in his arms. Now, Dex lived alone in an apartment above the bar. I wondered what had happened.

"La Bolsa Police." It was a gruff voice, a practiced one, as if to tell the caller, *For your sake this call better be worth our time.*

"Detective Branch."

"Who wants him?"

"Liam Sol. He'll want to talk to me. Get him now."

There was a long silence on the other end. Christ. Were they trying to trace the call? Or was that just TV detective stuff? God, I didn't know shit. I couldn't give them much longer. I didn't have much time before the pale-faced guy found me.

Branch came on the line. "Sol, where are you?"

"He's after me. He took my truck."

"Who? Your mystery man?"

"Branch, goddammit, just listen." I took a breath. "He's following me. He's got my truck." I knew I had to tell him where I was. "I'm at the DMZ now, but I'm leaving. He's here. Just get him, and I'll turn myself in. I promise you that."

"Stay there, Sol. Don't move."

"Get here now. You get him, you get me."

I slammed the phone down and left Dex's office. I walked out to the bar and froze. The scent of black clove cigarettes filled the air, and a trace of smoke drifted over the bar.

"Dex?"

I stepped toward the exit. My gun pointed at nothing and everything. Then I saw him. He was slumped over the bar, eyes wide open, a trail of blood leaking out from the gaping slash on his neck. A black cigarette stub burned in the ashtray next to him. I scanned the room, ready to pull the trigger. Why didn't he kill me right here in the DMZ? I knew what he was doing. He was toying with me. The sick fuck wanted me to suffer. God, I wanted to kill him. I heard sirens. Branch was moving fast. I looked at Dex: another killing on me. I had to find the pale-faced guy—or he would find me. Either way, I had to be ready. I scrambled out of the bar and into a night filled with burning hillsides and falling ash.

CHAPTER THIRTY-NINE

I GREW UP IN this town. As a kid I played hide and seek in the downtown countless times. I knew more hiding places than anyone. But everything was different now. I felt like an unwanted visitor. The pale-faced guy was always one step ahead of me. I wondered if he knew me better than I knew myself.

I skirted along the darkest part of Main and turned into an alley behind the La Bolsa Surf Shop. I tried to stay in the darkness of the shadows, but still I felt like I had a spotlight on me. The pale-faced man could have killed me earlier today. If he could shoot a sea lion from that distance, he could have easily put a bullet into my forehead. No, he was taunting me. He could find me anytime he wanted; he was just choosing his moment.

The sirens stopped. I was sure they were at the DMZ now, examining Dex's body. Branch was telling his troops that I was armed and dangerous. Everyone loved Dex. I could hear them. They were pissed off. The cops were on the street, looking for me—a human target now—their fingers tensed on the triggers of their guns.

I slipped into a narrow passageway between the Gold Coast and the Bill Monroe Insurance Agency that led to an abandoned Enco gas station. The side door was unlocked, and I crept inside. The overpowering scent of stale oil and old urine battled for supremacy. The reek of the vintage piss seemed to be holding the winning edge. When I was a kid we used to fill our bike tires up here, and then we'd buy Double Colas from the cooler. The painting of the Enco Tiger and the slogan "Put a Tiger in Your Tank" was still visible on one of the walls. It struck me as ironic that with all the oil being pumped out of the ground, somehow this gas station went out of business.

Through the grease-stained window, I saw the red light of a cop car race by. This was a bad place to stay. I needed to find a safer place, a place where I could catch my breath and think about my next move.

I remembered the old military bunkers that were built in World War II to protect the coastline from attacks by the Germans or Japanese. I knew the police would search for me there as it was an obvious place to hide. There was a small oil field about two blocks away. It would be dark there, and I'd be hard to find. The field sat next to the high school, and I doubted it had much oil left to give. But my dad would draw every ounce of crude from the ground before giving it up for development. Just like the coffee commercial, he'd said his wells were "good to the last drop."

I climbed a chain-linked fence behind the gas station and took a shortcut through some backyards. It was late, but as I slipped by the windows, it appeared as if each house had someone stationed in front of their TV set, watching the flames roar in black and white, waiting to see if the fires would overtake the town. No one would be sleeping tonight.

The oil field held six wells that drew out the crude. They whined as if they had little strength left to make it through another night. I sat down and leaned against the base of one of the wells. I pulled out my gun and checked the bullets. My hand no longer shook, but the pistol felt heavy and wrong, like something I had stolen but would never be able to return.

Sirens blared as the police cars hunted me through the streets. They weren't being discreet. They were making a point. They wanted me to know that my time was running short. I held on to the gun and closed my eyes. I wasn't sleepy, but with my eyes shut I could see Dawn, alive, smiling, reaching for me. It was only a vision. But in it, she was alive and we were together. I didn't know how long I sat there. Judging by the position of the moon, its glow seeping out through the clouds of smoke, it must have been a couple of hours. I stood up to stretch my arms. I hadn't heard a siren in a while, but that didn't mean much. They were waiting for sunrise, when I'd be easier to find, when I'd be an easier target.

Then I saw him. The pale-faced man was on the pier, standing under one of the lights, as if he were on stage, performing for an audience of one. It was time. Time to confront the pale-faced man. Time to come face-to-face with the man who was calling me out to my execution. I'd read somewhere that soldiers found a sense of calm when going out on a suicide mission. Maybe it was because they knew the outcome was predetermined. Or maybe you become calm when you've run out of choices and you know there's only one way out. I didn't know the reason, but whatever calmness I felt was laced with a sense of fear and loneliness that seeped into my entire being. The combination was nothing I could explain. Nothing I understood. What I did know was that only one of us was going to come out of this alive.

As I began to climb the fence, I felt a light touch on my shoulder.

"Don't go," she said, her eyes dark and filled with tears.

I turned to her, wanting her to be real, but then she vanished. Yet the familiar scent of plumeria followed me down to the ocean.

CHAPTER FORTY

THE PALE-FACED MAN

HE WATCHED AS the surfer tried to sneak his way up to the pier. The surfer walked low, his head down, trying to keep to the shadows, stopping behind trees, walls, and trash cans, whatever he could find. The theory was sound, but the execution a joke. This guy wouldn't last long in a war zone.

He thought back on Vietnam. He knew of some who claimed that their experience in the war had damaged them. But Nam hadn't damaged him; it had defined him. It made life clear; it gave him purpose. It gave him the permission to kill. And he was good at it, too good. While others received medals for going above and beyond the call of duty, when he did it, they pinned him with a dishonorable discharge. To his chagrin he learned that the U.S. Army didn't understand the nature of war at all.

Even those who hired him didn't truly understand what needed to be done. But he knew. The only good way to fix a problem was to eliminate it. He should have killed the surfer right away. All the trouble the guy had caused would never have occurred if he had just taken him out at the beginning. Finally, now, he would fix the problem once and for all.

The surfer waded into the water. The pale-faced man could see that he carried a gun. This was going to be interesting. The pale-faced man lit up a cigarette and scanned the pier for a dark place where he could sit and wait, a place where he would be in control.

CHAPTER FORTY-ONE

I TOOK THE LONG way around, through side streets and alleys. I wanted to approach the pier from the north so I'd be out of his direct line of sight. When I got to the water's edge, I walked under the structure to keep from being seen. The pier creaked with the pull of the tide. I waded through the water, keeping the gun above my head, feeling my way along the pilings to keep my balance. The water was unnaturally warm, as if the fire in the hills had caused it to simmer. I stopped just below where the Sea Legs Bar was located on the pier. There was a tiny space behind it where they kept their trash cans.

When I was a kid, my friends and I used to climb these pilings whenever we played pirates. I tucked my gun into my jeans and started to make my way up. The grooves in the wood aided my climb, but my hands and fingers found all the splinters. As they dug into my skin, the blood dripped freely into the water below. My hands were raw by the time I had made it to the railing. I slipped over the rail and crouched down behind the Sea Legs, waiting until I could catch my breath. My clothes were weighted down from all the water, so I shed them, leaving only my boxers on.

If he had stayed where he was, I thought I'd be able to sneak up on him. I crept along the side of the Sea Legs Bar. I stopped, said a silent prayer, and then sprinted out to the open, gun drawn, ready to fire. I turned quickly, scanning the pier, but he was gone.

I stood alone in the middle of the La Bolsa pier, barefoot, in my wet boxers, with a Colt Cobra .38 Special in my hand, the cock pulled all the way back.

I didn't know what to do. I knew he was watching me, my presence no longer a secret. I edged back toward the Sea Legs, and then I heard him, breathing hard, almost as if he were having sex. I held the gun tightly, my finger on the trigger, and swung around. Nothing. I caught a flicker above me, and then a lit cigarette butt landed at my feet. A dark figure crouched on the roof of the Sea Legs above me. He leaped off the roof, flying toward me like a bird of prey. I raised the Cobra, but it was too late. The air rushed from my lungs as he landed on top of me; the gun flew from my hand. The pale-faced man had pinned my arms to the ground. He laughed in my ear, and I smelled the sickly scent of the clove cigarettes on his breath.

He looked down at me, licking his lips. "Why didn't you just back off?" he said, his voice wet and thick as if coated in motor oil. "I wasn't supposed to kill anyone. It's all your fault, surfer boy. They all died because of you."

He moved his hands to my face, caressing my cheeks. He let out a high-pitched giggle, and then he squeezed my face hard. I felt like I was stuck in a vice, my jaws on the verge of snapping. "You know, I didn't want to kill your girlfriend. I didn't. You should have left well enough alone." He clenched his teeth. "She died because of you. I told her that, you know. I told her you were the one who killed her."

He pulled one of his hands loose and slapped me hard across the face.

"Why did you kill my father?"

He shook his head. "What are you talking about?"

He slapped me again and pushed his fingers deep into my throat. His mouth fell open, and bits of his drool dripped onto my face. I couldn't breathe. I flailed my arms around as if trying to tread water. I was drowning on dry land. I tried to gouge his eyes, but all I caught was air. He eased up on my throat and examined me for a moment, like I was some kind of lab experiment. There was a bruise on his left cheekbone. Dawn did that—I knew it. She had hurt him.

As if reading my mind, he gently rubbed his bruise and then pressed both his hands down on my throat, choking me. I shut my eyes and grabbed both of his little fingers and tried to pull them back. He was freakishly strong. Flashes of light exploded in front of my eyes like an electrical storm. I kept pulling. It felt like they were about to give. He grunted like a wounded animal, and then his fingers snapped. He pulled his hands free, which allowed me a second to take in some air. He threw a backhand to my face and grabbed my neck, again pushing deep into my throat. I found his ring fingers and gripped them and pulled them back. He knew what I was doing, but I kept pulling. The flashes of light began to fade. I had little time left. His fingers were slippery with sweat, but I wouldn't let go. I couldn't let go. Letting go would be my death. A tiny squeal slipped from his mouth, and then his fingers died in my hands just as they snapped.

"God damn you," he screamed. His voice high, like a little girl's. He let go of my throat, transfixed by his broken fingers.

I clasped my hands together in a fist and swung at his jaw. The impact rocked him just enough to give me some room to crawl out from under him. I scrambled to my feet, scanning the pier for the gun. I couldn't see it anywhere. I prayed it hadn't fallen into the ocean.

He got to his feet and stared at his hands as if he couldn't believe what I'd done to them. Drool dripped from his parted lips. He locked his eyes on mine, growling like a rabid dog, his face contorted and hideous. I needed to get the hell out of there, but my feet wouldn't move.

He lurched toward me, running blindly. I took a wild swing at him and caught him on the nose. It shattered, blood spilling from his nostrils, but it didn't slow him. He tackled me, my skull hitting hard against the ground. Slivers of shattered light exploded in front of me. He was striking me with what was left of his fists, the blood from his busted nose gushing over me.

I raised my hands, trying to defend myself. I blocked some of the punches, but some still found their way to my face. I searched for something, anything that could help me. I spotted a life preserver on the side of the rail above me. I couldn't take my eyes off it. I realized that the water was my life preserver. I had to get into the water. I reached for the bottom rail and tried to pull myself under and into the waves below, but there was nothing left in my arms. They were dead. He saw what I was trying to do, and he dragged me back to him. From the corner of my eye, I could see waves of fire tearing through the hillsides. His last punch rocked me so hard that I felt my eyes roll back into my head. Then I saw the gun, within arm's length, teetering on the edge of the pier.

I couldn't let him see it. I needed a diversion. I locked my eyes on his and started laughing in his face like a madman. He didn't know what to make of my reaction. He quit throwing punches and tilted his head. He looked like a rabid version of the RCA Records dog. I grabbed the gun. I heard police sirens approach and the sounds of tires skidding to a stop.

I heard a familiar voice yelling from far away. "Sol! Sol!"

I pointed the gun at the killer's face, his expression one of complete confusion as I pulled the trigger.

The wail of the police sirens couldn't drown out the thunder of the gunshot. The pale-faced guy was there, and then he wasn't. It was that quick. The smell of gunpowder hung in the air, and I felt pieces of him rain down on me. Red lights flashed in the smoke-filled sky. He wasn't there, but I couldn't stop firing. I'd lost control. I kept pulling the trigger until long after the last bullet left its chamber.

"Sol. Sol. It's okay. It's over." Detective Branch took the gun from me and then held my hand. "It's over, Sol. You got him. He's dead."

I closed my eyes and cried. I wanted my father. I wanted Dawn back. I wanted to feel safe again.

CHAPTER FORTY-TWO

We were in Detective Branch's office, and I had just given my statement. He sat at his desk and stared into an empty Styrofoam cup.

They let me wash off the blood and change clothes. They gave me a La Bolsa PD T-shirt and an old pair of swim trunks to wear.

"Whose swim trunks are these?"

"They were from a drowning victim a few months back."

"You're kidding?"

Branch shook his head. "He's not going to miss them, believe me."

He threw the Styrofoam cup into the trash.

My face hurt like a bitch. I was going to have to see a doctor, but I figured he'd just inflict more pain on me. And I was in no condition for that now.

"I'm tempted to lock you up, you know."

"You're thinking of arresting me?"

Branch didn't answer.

"You got the guy. What else do you need? He's in no shape to sign a confession."

"I don't like loose ends. But from what you told me, and what we saw tonight, let's just say that maybe I believe your story. Maybe." He shook his head. "Christ, you left quite a fuckin' mess for us to clean up. Do you even have a permit for that gun?"

"A permit? What the hell?"

Branch observed me with what, for him, must have been an expression of sympathy. He saw that I was still shaking from the incident. "You'll get over it."

"You ever kill anyone before?" I asked.

"No." He glanced down at his shoes. "Well, I've heard you get over it. Listen, it was either him or you."

"We still need to identify this guy," Greene said. "We didn't find a thing on him."

"I bet Dane Lohan knew him," I said. "I don't know why, but he and Dane were in on this."

"But we still don't know who he is, or how Lohan knew him. But we'll find out. I just don't get it. Did Lohan have him kill your father, or did this guy discover that Lohan murdered your father and was blackmailing *him*? Maybe they were in business together. Maybe Dane arrested him once." He eyed Greene. "We're going to need to examine Lohan's files."

Detective Greene glared at me. I couldn't tell if he thought I was the guilty one or not.

I shrugged. Too many thoughts raced through my head. One was that the pale-faced man admitted to killing Dawn, but not my father. I didn't let Branch in on that as I feared that would be getting too close to home.

"I'll have Detective Greene give you a ride back. Just don't leave town. We're going to have more questions for you."

"You know where I live."

Branch smiled and told me there were no hard feelings. I told him to go fuck himself and walked out the door.

CHAPTER FORTY-THREE

THE MORNING SUN squinted through the black and orange sky. It looked like sunset in reverse. But the smell from the fire had eased up.

"The winds shifted," Detective Greene said. "We're going to be all right."

I wanted to laugh at the absurdity of his statement, but I felt like crying because I knew nothing was ever going to be all right again. But I also knew from my years on the water that the wind could change direction again without notice.

We made our way down Pacific Coast Highway in a patrol car. Greene had the siren going, and I could tell he loved having cars pull over to the side of the road for him.

"What's your partner's problem?"

"He doesn't like you."

"I know that. He seemed pissed that I wasn't the killer."

"You are in a way. If it weren't for you, Dawn would still be alive." He echoed the words the killer had said to me. The same thing I'd told myself countless times.

He bit his lip. "Branch saved her once, you know."

I felt my mouth drop open.

"You didn't know?"

But I realized I did know. Dawn had told me the story. When she was eight years old some pervert had tried to pull her into his car.

"Right outside of Johnny-Bob's Donuts," Greene said. "Branch was off duty, having a coffee and a maple bar. He sees this guy dragging a girl into a car. Branch runs out and fights the guy off."

"Anyway, he takes the guy back to the station and we print him. A few calls to other stations and we were able to link this guy to other killings up and down the coast. All of the victims were young girls. All of them raped and murdered."

I couldn't remember Dawn ever mentioning the name of the cop who had saved her.

"He didn't keep in touch with her after that. He was just doing his job—it's what we do—but he kept his eye out for her, you know. As bad as it got for him—and it got bad… divorce, drinking—he always had that. He had saved a young girl's life. He'd done something good. He mattered. That was something you could never take from him."

For the life of me, I couldn't think of one good thing I'd ever done. There must have been something, but at the moment, I was at a loss.

The next few miles we rode in silence. Even though the waves were choppy from the wind, there were still a few surfers out there. Mexico sounded nice. It always sounded nice. Mexico was my refuge, a place I always ran to when life became too much for me to handle.

"Let me ask you something," Greene said. "What would you be doing if your daddy wasn't rich and connected?"

I shook my head. Hell, I didn't know.

"You'd be in Nam."

I looked at Greene.

"You ever get a draft notice?"

My look must have given away the answer.

"You think that was all just dumb luck?"

Greene stopped for the light at Canyon Road. I got out of the car. I didn't need to hear any more of this guy's shit, no matter how true it may have been.

"Where are you going?"

"I can walk from here."

As I crossed the highway, I heard Greene's patrol car peel out and race back toward La Bolsa, his siren screaming. Then I headed toward my parents' house for what I was sure would be the last time.

CHAPTER FORTY-FOUR

IT WAS A long walk to the house. I thought about hitching a ride, but with my face bruised, battered, and swollen, I doubted anyone would dare pick me up. The walk would give me time to think, time to figure things out. The killings had started in the family. Christ, the whole town of La Bolsa started with my family. Who didn't we touch?

I felt the rush of the cars as they whipped by. The changing wind had cleared the air, making it easier to breathe, making it easier to see. I followed the last flurries of smoke and ash toward home, back to where the killings had begun.

The house, of course, had been left untouched by the flames. The fires seemed to have stopped at the property line. My family even had an influence over nature.

The house was quiet. From the kitchen I could see my mother on the back patio, staring out at the charred hillsides.

I stepped outside onto the patio. "Fires just missed you, didn't they?"

She didn't move.

"Surprised I'm here?"

She slowly turned to me. Her face pale, tears welling up in her eyes.

"I thought… I thought—"

"You thought what?"

"I don't know what I thought. Looks like you've been in quite a row. Come inside. We'll get some ice on that."

She walked past me and I followed her back into the kitchen.

"Did you do it?" I asked.

"What? What are you talking about?"

"They think they caught his killer, Mom." My voice cracked. "He's dead. I killed him. You're off the hook."

I saw the sense of relief in her eyes. "You killed him?"

"And you killed Dad."

"You've been through a lot. You don't know what you're saying."

"The two of you had gotten into a fight. He walked out. You were the only one who knew where he would go. Just like he always did after one of your fights, he went to the pier."

"You're talking nonsense."

"Am I? Tell me about Joy Kiyan."

Her expression grew hard.

"I don't get it. You must have known for a long time that Dad was her father."

Her hands shook. She held them together as tightly as she could, but still they kept shaking.

"He was obsessed with that woman," she said. "Then when that bastard child was born… it felt as if he'd never loved me. He thought I didn't know about her, the fool."

She stared at the hills through the window. "I should have killed him after what he did to Isabelle. I should have killed him then. There were a million times since then that he deserved to die."

She turned back to me.

"You killed him?" I asked.

"I wish I had. Is that what you want to hear?"

"It wasn't Mom, Liam."

Marie stood in the doorway. Her eyes were bloodshot, and it appeared as if she'd been crying.

"What do you mean? You killed him?"

"No, Liam. Sorry to disappoint you, but it wasn't me."

"But you know who did it."

"It was dear Isabelle. Could you blame her, Liam, after what he did to her?"

"She wasn't here that night. She was in Brentwood."

Marie looked at me the way you'd look at a puppy that you were trying to housebreak. "That was the story we gave. She was here, Liam. Glenn was in San Diego, so she spent the night with us. She followed Felix out to the pier that night and killed him."

"She walked right in here and told us that she killed him. I had no idea that she'd even left the house," my mother said.

"Isabelle told us the whole story," Marie continued. "She told us what she had done as if she were describing a simple trip to the grocery store." Marie folded her arms in front of her chest as if a cold breeze had found her. "She's not who you think she is."

"Don't blame this on her." *God, not Isabelle*, I thought. My father wasn't the only one in the family who'd hurt her.

"Liam, you never liked reality, did you?" Marie said. "Always running off to the waves."

"I don't believe you." But it made perfect sense. Isabelle had every right to kill him. I just didn't want it to be her. "Where is she?"

I caught the glance my mother and Marie shared.

"Where is she?"

"I'm getting something for that eye of yours," my mother said.

"She's someplace safe, Liam. She needs more help than we can provide her."

"What have you done to her?"

"Nothing, Liam," Marie said. "We're protecting her."

"From whom?"

"From herself," my mother responded. She handed me ice wrapped in a dish towel.

The ice made the side of my face feel like the bite from a jellyfish. "She did your dirty work for you, didn't she?"

"What are you talking about?" my mother asked.

"You both wanted him dead. For different reasons, maybe, but you both wanted Dad out of the way."

My mother started to respond, but Marie stopped her.

"Isabelle acted on her own free will. We had to respond quickly, and we had to be smart about it. But, yes, certain advantages opened up for us when he died."

"You're glad he's dead. I can't believe this."

"How dare you, Liam!" my mother screamed as she came at me. Marie grabbed her and held her back.

"Do you know why Isabelle killed him? Do you?" Marie asked. "She was trying to protect you. You didn't know that, did you? Isabelle wanted to save you from him. She was worried what Felix was going to turn you into."

Marie eyed me with a mix of cruelty and pity. "You, working for him? What a joke. Especially after all I had done for Felix. Poor Isabelle, she thought she was saving you."

"But you wanted me out of the way, too. That crazy fuck was going after me, and you guys did nothing." I focused my eyes on Marie. "You hired him, right?"

"Felix always used cousin Carlos to scare people off, but we couldn't very well use him this time. He would have turned us all in. Dane found this guy. We never even met him. He was supposed to take care of Eddie Capuano, but then Dane told the guy to scare you off after you kept after him with all your questions. But you didn't back off, and Dane couldn't control him. And after he killed himself—"

"You mean after the guy murdered Dane."

"We don't know that, Liam. Anyway, we couldn't stop him. We didn't know where to find him. Dane had arranged everything."

"You could have called the police. You could have—"

My mother glared at me. "And then what?" The coldness in her voice was like nothing I had ever heard. "We'd all be in jail. Why didn't you just back off? No one would have died other than that useless drunkard Eddie Capuano, and no one was going to miss him, not even his parents. You're the cause of it all. Why didn't you do what you've always done before? Why couldn't you have just done nothing?"

I threw the towel down. The ice scattered across the floor. I was seeing them, my sister and my mother, for the first time.

"Someone killed my father. I wanted to know why. I didn't think my own family would be behind it. Why didn't you tell me the truth?"

"We didn't think you'd be able to handle it," Marie said. "So, I went to Dane. I knew he'd do anything for me. We were going to keep it clean. Don't look at me like that. He arranged for the guy to deal with Eddie. It was done. Just another junkie taking his own life. Everything was fine. No loose ends. Then you started asking questions. We told you to leave it alone, but you kept at it."

"He killed Dawn. She wasn't part of this."

Marie shook her head. "Dane hired a madman, the idiot." She gritted her teeth. "We could have protected you."

"By putting me in jail?"

"We would have thought of something, Liam. I am the power around here now."

"You could have fooled me."

I sank into one of the chairs, my face buried in my hands. It felt like a scene right out of *The Outer Limits* mixed with *Peyton Place*: my mother giving me ice to mend a wound after my sister kills my father and my family sends a hit man out to kill me.

"So, going after the Kiyans' land, that was all some kind of revenge for Dad cheating on you."

"Do you know how much that land is worth?" Marie asked. "A strawberry farm, are you kidding me?"

"Dad took care of their land when they were interned."

"Christ, they should have sent them all back to Japan after the war. He rubbed his affair with that woman in Brona's face. Once Glenn is elected, we can move to rezone the land and get them out for good."

"That guy went after them, too. He put Joy in the hospital. You had him go after the Kiyans?"

"Dane asked him to deal with the Kiyans. Two for one."

"That guy could have killed her."

"How many times do you have to hear it? We couldn't stop him. We didn't know how."

"I can't believe you had Dane sic that guy on them, too. You knew Mrs. Kiyan was going to fight you. And you couldn't have that. The truth about Joy would have come out."

Marie gave me a hard look. "We gave them a fair offer on the land. They should have accepted it."

"Holy Christ. Who are you people?"

"This world's just too big for you, Liam," Marie said. "You have no idea how things really work."

I looked at my mother. She was staring off into the nightmare that was her life. "I loved your father, you know. Through it all, somehow, I loved him. We had to protect Isabelle. He put her through so much. We had to protect Isabelle."

"Where is she?"

My mom shook her head.

"You can't go to her, Liam. It will set everything back," Marie said. "We want her to forget what happened."

"So she won't go to the police, you mean."

"No, Liam. So she can have a life," my sister replied. "Do you want her to spend the rest of her life in prison? Is that what you want?"

"No," I said.

"Good. She's safe now, Liam. No one can hurt her, and you can't help her."

"I want to see her. I think I can help."

I turned to my Mother, but she shook her head.

"Liam," my mom said. She extended her arms to me.

I walked over to my mother and gave her a hug and kissed her forehead. She smelled of flowers and Irish whiskey. I thought of all the times she had taken care of me. The times she'd tucked me in. How proud of me she'd been when I scored my first basket in a game. I thought of everything she did for me, and then I felt it all slip away.

"Do you forgive me, Liam?"

When I didn't respond, she said, "Liam, please tell me you forgive me."

"I can't, Mother," I whispered, my voice cracking. "I can't."

I felt her body shudder in my arms as she started to cry.

I kissed her again, and her arms dropped to her side.

"Don't go, Liam. We're your family. You can't leave us," my mother said as she tried to fight back the tears.

"You're not going to the police, are you, Liam? They won't believe you," Marie shouted.

"Liam," my mother said, "for the love of God, please don't go."

Part of me wanted to come back to her. I knew if I stopped walking, that I'd never leave. I'd hold on to my mother and wouldn't let go.

"Liam," she wailed. "Liam!" Her screams tore at my heart.

As I walked out the front door, I could hear Marie yelling, drowning out my mother's pleas. "They won't believe you. I'm cutting you out, Liam. You hear me? No more free ride."

I kept walking. My tears made it difficult to see, but I knew where I was going. I headed down the driveway, past the citrus trees and the places we used to hide as kids—these were the places where we'd felt most safe in this world, but they were all covered in ash now, faded memories of a time and a place that no longer existed.

I stood at the end of the driveway. The Pacific Ocean lay beyond me. It looked deep and blue and beautiful and forgiving. It seemed as alien to me as an undiscovered galaxy.

I hitched a ride. As soon as the teenage boy driving the car saw my face, he made me sit in the back of his El Camino. I crawled in next to his surfboard, which was banged up as all hell, as if every ride he had ever attempted had ended in a bone-crushing wipeout. As we drove along the coast, I saw dozens of surfers sitting on the bluffs, looking out over the ocean, their backs to the world, their boards next to them like tombstones. The onshore winds had blown out the waves, leaving behind a messy and ragged body of water, but the surfers were patient. They knew that everything could change in an instant. I had him drop me off at Ocean and PCH. There was one last place I wanted to visit.

"Dawn Elizabeth Arnett, Loving Daughter." I sat next to her grave, Indian style, like we used to do when we'd sit on the beach and talk through the night. I still couldn't find the words. I didn't think there were any, not adequate ones, anyway. Not to the one true person who had made me believe I could be anything—but in the end I not only failed her belief in me, but I failed myself. Sometimes it really is too late, because some actions can never be redeemed.

In that moment, I didn't know who I was crying for, but one time we had a dream, a beautiful dream. A dream that brought me comfort. A dream that I thought would wait patiently for me while I rode impossible waves that would never end.

EPILOGUE

I RECEIVED A LETTER from Isabelle the other day. She mailed it four months ago. She was still upset that I had enlisted, but she said that she understood. She was doing better now. Isabelle said that she could almost forget what had happened to her. I knew that wasn't true. It would never be true. The ink had bled a little from what I was sure were her tearstains. I read her words again. This time more slowly. She was never going to forget. If you took all the pain from her, then there would be nothing left. I folded the letter and secured it in my pocket. She was back with my family again, and they weren't going to let her go. She knew too much. *I won't forget you, Isabelle.* I made the sign of the cross and said a prayer for her.

I thought of my father. What he was to me. What he was to Isabelle. What he was to my mother, Marie, and Mrs. Kiyan. What he was to La Bolsa. I hated him, but found, shamefully, that I couldn't help but love him, too. That I still wanted him to be proud of me. That I wanted to be the person he'd thought I could be, though I never wanted to be anything like him. No matter how hard I tried, I knew I would never understand how I could still love such an evil man.

You don't just pay for your own sins; you pay for the sins of others.

Nothing, I realized, is ever free. We pay more than we're ever worth. And once you know what you owe, the payments never seem to end. Whoever said that the truth shall set you free didn't know what the hell they were talking about.

"Move out."

The thunderclouds that stalked us from above opened up. The storms came every day, and you could never get used to them. I pulled the hood of my poncho over my head, grabbed my M16, and caught up with my platoon as we trudged through the jungle and into another impending firefight. Most of the time I found myself shooting at shadows. Shadows that wanted nothing more than to see me die. It was a typical start to each new day. Maybe this time a bullet would find me, but something told me that wasn't going to happen. It's what you don't know that can kill you, and control is only an illusion. No, I was being pushed by that never-ending swell, and all I could do was hold on until it dumped me off on a beach somewhere of its own choosing, leaving me alone in the wet sand, daring me to come back into the water for one more ride.

Made in the USA
San Bernardino, CA
22 February 2017